IDK!

IDK!

Ramona L Thomas, M.Ed.

Copyright © 2023 Ramona L Thomas, M.Ed.

All rights reserved. This book or any portion thereof may not be reproduced or used in any manner whatsoever without the express written permission of the publisher except for the use of brief quotations in a book review.

For my princess, Christinah Fatona

Those who have no record of what their forebears have accomplished lose the inspiration which comes from the teaching of biography and history.

—Carter G. Woodson

Table of Contents

Introduction · xi
Acknowledgments · xiii

1   Food Origin · 1
2   Heads or Tails · 10
3   Trick Question? · 17
4   Win By Two · 24
5   What Is Soul Food · 31
6   Manny vs Money · 41
7   Grandad Says · 45
8   The 1800's · 59
9   Road Trip · 69
10 Welcome Back! · 77
11 The First Humans! · 87
12 Less Than 24 Hours · 95
13 International Day · 109
14 The Speeches · 118

About the Author · 129
Discussion Questions · 130

Kyndle's Family Recipes · 132
Collard Greens · 133
Sweet Potato Pie · 134
Black-Eyed Peas · 136
Cornbread · 137
Red Beans and Rice · 138
Okra and Tomatoes · 140
Rice · 142
Hot Water Corn Bread · 143

Introduction

THE AMERICAN STORY of Soul food has been brewing inside me for several years. After writing my first book, *Grandma's Brown Cookies*, I was invited to several schools throughout the San Francisco Bay Area to read excerpts from my book. Sometimes the students would ask me if I'd written other books. I would let them know that I'd coauthored a book about language and the importance of code switching. Inevitably the next question would be: "What will your next story be about?"

I would answer, "Soul food. Can anyone tell me what it is?"

Blank stares often permeated the classrooms. The students were of various ethnicities (Black, Mexican, Filipino, Indian, Chinese, Vietnamese, and others). It saddened me when no answers came forth. I was bothered by their lack of knowledge about Black American cuisine. I was not surprised when many of the non-Black students couldn't answer my question, but I was disappointed when Black students didn't attempt to answer either. I thought, *Surely they've eaten collard greens, black-eyed peas, corn bread, and other dishes from our delicious cuisine.* I wondered if no one had answered because they were bashful or if they truly didn't know the answer.

Without linkage to a specific country, Soul food appears homeless. The fact of the matter is, Soul food does have a home, and it always has. This experience, among others, confirms for me the importance of telling the story of the emergence of Soul food. Shortly after Hurricane Katrina, I went to the local beauty college to get a manicure. As the Korean manicurist filed my nails, we chitchatted. She mentioned she had recently come to California via Mississippi and expressed how much she loved Mississippi cuisine. This prompted me to ask her, "Which foods do you like?" After she named some of her favorite dishes, I stated, "Oh, you like Black American food."

Her response was, "I didn't know it was Black American food. I like American food." Bingo! Soul food is American food.

I was more determined than ever to share the legacy of Soul food. I fear that if the evolution of Soul food isn't taught, it will be buried among many historical facts that pertain to the history of Blacks in America. Food brings people of various ethnicities together. It not only nourishes the body, it nourishes the soul!

Acknowledgments

To those who have supported me on my journey to getting this story finished, thank you! To my Soulmate, Keith Nickens, I will always appreciate you for being close and giving me the space I need to be at my best. To my parents, Elbert and Ella Thomas, I hope the internet is in heaven, so you can cherish and share this story with our heavenly family and friends. To my daughter Christinah Fatona, thank you for giving me the tea on the T. To my son, Kyndle Nickens, thank you for helping me bring voice to the characters and make the content relevant. Myila Granberry, you always think of me when opportunities arise for book sales. Invitations to Mills College and discussions with OUSD staff and students have been rewarding. Keep 'em coming! Sybil Carter Love, I look forward to attending many more Juneteenth celebrations. Christell Grace, you have your finger on the pulse of what matters to young students; your connection to them helped bring *IDK!* to life. Stacey Bristow, your quick eye gave birth to the chapter subtitles; thank you. To Jonathan Carmargo, my beta reader, your input let me know readers have a keen interest in learning this aspect of American history. Camille Tompkins, I always enjoy hearing your point of view. Elizabeth Dangelantonio, our chance meeting on an Alaskan cruise proved to be a godsend. Your kindness, attention to detail, and willingness to critique my work will forever be a blessing to me. Chris Sharpe II, thank you for your creativity and patience. Jaylynn St. Julian, thank you for hosting one of my early book signings; I look forward to your continued support. As a writer, it's easy for me to overlook my mistakes. Lara Williams, having your second pair of eyes to proofread the final version of my work was essential. I was thrilled to learn you found very few mistakes. Thank you. Deborah Day, thank you for promoting my books. Because of you, my work is now in the hands of students all across America. All of your input has helped to shape IDK! My heartfelt thanks goes out to you. My hope is that Soul food will no longer be considered a common noun, but that it takes its rightful place as the proper noun it so deserves, and its rightful place in the history of American cuisine.

1

Food Origin
Friday after Class

While I wait for Miss Fatona to return to the classroom, my cell phone beeps. It's Tinah. She's texting me:

"I overheard yo' so-called friends throwin' shade, talkin' 'bout how dumb you looked."

Reading her words gets me heated.

Quickly I reply, "Who's throwin' shade? I'm in the classroom, still waiting to talk to Miss Fatona."

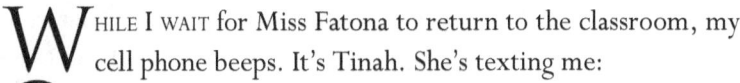
She keeps texting, "Fola and nem was ROFL."

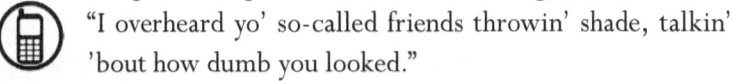
Where did you see em?

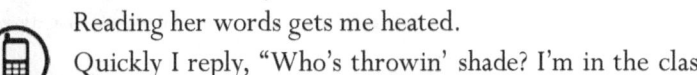
"By Krishna's locker. They were so busy crackin' up and gossipin', they didn't see me and Maria."

"We caught some of what they was sayin' 'bout you."

📱 "Fola said, 'Man, I can't believe he was slipping like that. He's s'posed to be smart and couldn't answer that easy question. That was hella funny."

📱 "Somebody else said, 'Kyndle is not as smart as he thinks he is,' but I didn't see who said it. One of 'em said, 'Yep, he has no common sense."

📱 I definitely heard Tony say, 'He look dumb, just sitting there. I feel sorry for him.' When I saw Krishna running his mouth, I just knew he was talkin' 'bout you.

📱 He said, "Lower your voices," when he saw me and Maria.

📱 It was too late, we already heard 'em.

📱 They didn't know we overheard 'em talkin' 'bout you, because we played it cool when we approached them. I said to Krishna, 'Spill the tea.'

📱 I hear Miss Fatona wrapping up her hallway conversation. She's telling Miss Granberry, "See you later," so I quickly text Tinah, "I gotta go."

📱 She text, "HMU"
K.

I put my phone back inside my pocket.

Tinah's text messages have me fuming. I suspected Krishna and Fola would have something to say; they can be so petty. This feels like the worst day of my life.

After reading Tinah's text messages, I begin recalling what happened.

Yesterday and Earlier Today

Holding a yellow permission slip in her hand, Miss Fatona said, "Be sure to have this signed by a parent or guardian."

She continued, "For our International Day celebration, I'm asking each of you to bring your cultural food dish that serves up to ten people or more. Your report and speech will be about the food you're bringing, and you'll present to the entire school. Make sure the food you're sharing is listed on the permission slip. We'll discuss decorations later."

Tinah raised her hand asking, "Are our parents allowed to come?"

"Yes Tinah, this will be a community heritage celebration. All families are welcome."

After the permission slips were turned in Miss Fatona said, "When I call your name, state what food you're bringing and its origin."

Miss Fatona called, "Kiko."

"To clarify, you want us to name where the food we're bringing for International Day originated?"

"That's right, Kiko."

I'm thinking, is this for real. I've never even thought about the origin of my cultural food. I definitely don't recall anybody in my family talking about it. As a matter of fact, I don't recall Miss Fatona saying we needed to have this information. *Did I miss something? I know I'm not slipping.*

Kiko can be such a show-off; she sat erect in her seat with perfect posture, then answered, "I'm bringing sashimi. The origin is Japan."

Miss Fatona continued calling names:

"Jose Gonzalez."

Jose adjusted his body, cleared his throat, and told us, "I'm bringing enchiladas with mole sauce. It's from Mexico, and it's *delicioso!*"

Fola said he was bringing some kind of special rice. I don't remember the name, but anyway, he was talkin' 'bout how he was bringing two huge pots.

Krishna was bringing tandoori chicken with naan, and he said, "It's from India."

Everybody answers the question with no problem. I really don't remember the question being assigned.

Pierre had the whole class cracking up when he raised both hands like a referee to get Miss Fatona's attention.

When she acknowledged him, he squirmed in his seat asking if he could go to the bathroom.

Before Miss Fatona allowed him to leave, she said, "Answer the question, then you can go."

With lighting speed Pierre said, "I'm bringing crepes. They are from France," then he rushed out the door, crisscrossing his legs like a race walker, trying not to pee on himself.

While everyone burst out laughing I sat quietly, trying to think of what I should say.

As soon as Miss Fatona regained control of the class, "Settle down, settle down," she called my name: "Kyndle."

"Can I go last?"

With a surprised look on her face, Miss Fatona said, "Okay. Maria, tell us the origin of the food you're bringing?"

"*Whew.*" I sighed with relief.

The more my classmates answered, the more I wanted to crawl under my desk.

Smoothing the jet-black bangs hovering over her eyes, Maria cleared her throat, "Ahem, ahem, and stated, "I'm bringing my mother's famous chicken adobo and *lumpia*. It's from the Philippines, and we have it for dinner at least once a week."

For some reason she looked at me, as though she was saying, *top that!*

Sometimes I can't stand Maria. She thinks everything is a competition. At that point I really wanted to escape, like a caged bird. I was so nervous!

"Kyndle."

Miss Fatona's bright-pink glossy lips were moving rapidly. "Blah, blah, blah, blah, blah, she asked, "Kyndle are you listening?"

"*Yeah.*" I snapped out of it.

My heart started beating faster: thump, thump, thump. I was so edgy. To buy more time I asked, "Can you repeat the question?"

She seemed ticked off when she had to repeat the question. In a stern, don't-play-with-me voice, she said, "State the origin of the food you're bringing for International Day. This is not intended to be a difficult question!"

I'm thinking, maybe not for anyone else, but clearly, I'm struggling. All eyes were on me. I could feel my shoulders beginning to slump as I placed one hand on my right leg to stop it from shaking.

With an annoyed look on her face, she asked, "Do you understand the question, Kyndle?"

"Yes, Miss Fatona. I understand."

"Then answer, young man. You've been given plenty of time," she commanded.

Like chattering teeth, my right leg was shaking. I took a deep breath to calm myself, but when I spoke, it wasn't loud enough. My voice cracked and was barely audible. Miss Fatona wasn't having it. "Speak up! We can't hear you," she demanded.

I repeated myself. "*I'm bringing...*"

"Louder, Kyndle. Why are you mumbling?"

Miss Fatona was really agitated.

I swallowed my saliva to moisten my mouth and spoke louder and clearer, "I'm bringing Soul food."

"Okay and the origin?"

It must have been apparent to everyone that I was struggling, especially Maria since she shot her hand straight up like a launched missile and tried to interrupt. Miss Fatona told her, "Hold your question; Kyndle isn't finished." She sighed as though exhausted before saying with compassion, "Go on, Kyndle."

With a heavy heart, I stared straight ahead, ensuring my eyes didn't connect with anyone and admitted, "I don't know."

Embarrassed, I continued staring at the whiteboard so my eyes wouldn't meet anyone else's, as I sensed all eyes on me.

Then the whispering started. "Wow! That was such an easy question."

"How'd he blow that one?"

"The nerd finally cracked. He thinks he's so smart, guess not."

"Wow, he's lame."

"Yeah, hella dumb."

I was heated! I stopped staring at the whiteboard, turned to look in the direction of the voices talking smack and giggling. I'm not dumb, I'm no slouch and they've got some nerves talking behind my back. Like I thought, they stopped when I looked directly at them.

Miss Fatona came to my rescue. "Quiet! There should be no side conversations."

Pesty Maria raised her hand again.

Appearing annoyed, Miss Fatona acknowledged Maria. "Yesss, Maria."

"Is Soul food from Seoul Korea?"

Quickly responding, Tinah started doin' extra, shaking her head and moving her arms like the rapper Cardi B. She blurted out, "Quit acting stupid, Maria. Does Kyndle look Korean?"

Miss Fatona doesn't play that! She warned Tinah, "No loud outbursts, young lady."

I was glad Tinah had my back, but felt bad that she got in trouble for it.

Jose and Tony sat in front of me, with their heads resting on their arms, while their bodies wiggled from laughing at me too. I think they thought they were being discreet. I wondered, *Why are my friends on my line like this?*

Miss Fatona warned everyone, "Be respectful."

Krishna started flinging his hand around to get Miss Fatona's attention.

"Krishna, do you want to say something?"

"My question is for Kyndle."

He turned around to look at me. "How is 'Soul' spelled? Is it S-O-U-L or S-E-O-U-L?"

"S-O-U-L," I said loud and clear. Krishna can be a pain.

Finally, Miss Fatona declared, "No more questions."

※

I felt relief at 2:50 p.m. when the bell chimed. I couldn't wait to get up outta there. It felt like a bad dream. Too bad it wasn't. Miss Fatona doled out more instructions and told me to see her after class. Before everyone dashed out, Miss Fatona stated, "It's important not to whisper when another student is speaking."

She continued admonishing the class for making fun while I struggled. "To those of you who snickered, giggled, or made an outburst when Kyndle was speaking, I strongly suggest that you consider apologizing. Let me give you all a bit of advice. Guide your life by the golden rule: 'Do unto others as you would have them do unto you.' Respectful behavior will take you far. It's best not to insult one classmate while attempting to support another. You're dismissed."

Miss Fatona stood near the classroom door as students bolted out. Next, she chatted with Miss Granberry, the math teacher whose classroom is across the hall. While Miss Fatona was outside the classroom, I read Tinah's text messages. When Miss Fatona stepped back into the classroom, she said, "What's going on, Kyndle?"

"Um, nothing."

IDK!

"I'm surprised that you couldn't name the origin of the food you're bringing."

"Sorry, I wasn't prepared because I didn't know we were expected to answer that question."

"Well, on a whim I decided to ask what I thought would be an easy, fun question to end our day. So don't feel bad. It was impromptu, and I did throw you guys a curveball."

Then she added, "Be sure to include the answer in your speech. I'm expecting quality work from you."

That was all she said.

Meeting over!

2

HEADS OR TAILS
Today after School

THE MEETING WAS no sweat. Tossing my backpack over my shoulder, I walk toward the door, relieved. "Bye, Miss Fatona."

"Enjoy your time off."

Dang, I forgot all about spring break beginning today. "You, too, Miss Fatona, enjoy your break."

Stepping into the empty hallway, I hit Tinah back on FaceTime. Her nose, eyes, and lips appear huge on my phone screen. Fully animated, her head moves around like a chicken as her free hand does somersaults while she talks.

She continues from where her text left off.

"Like I said, they didn't see me and Maria comin'. When I asked Krishna, 'What's the tea?' He was 'bout to say somethin' smart like: 'This is an A and B conversation, so C your way out!' but mid-sentence he changed and said, 'Um, nothing really.'

"Maria and I gave each other the *Oh, really* look! We didn't believe a word he was sayin'. Maria asked him, 'What were y'all talkin' about? Must be some juicy gossip since y'all huddled up and everything.'

Tryin' to bait him, I added, 'It's okay if y'all don't want to tell us. It's cool!' It didn't work though.

Fola ignored our questions too, and had the nerve to change the subject, telling us he's bringin' this dish called *jollof* rice. I ain't neva heard of no jollof rice until he mentioned it in class today, so I asked, 'What is it?'

"You know Fola; he couldn't wait to brag on his mama's cookin'. Talkin' 'bout, 'It's a scrummy Nigerian dish. My mother can burn, so I know you guys are going to love it.'

"Errbody busted out laughing when Tony mimicked Fola: 'Scrummy.'

"Kiko blasted him. 'You're in America now and still talking like you're in England.'

"Since Krishna and Pierre have family in Europe, they couldn't wait to come to Fola's defense: 'There's nothing wrong with saying scrummy.'

"That's right!" Fola bumped his fist against Krishna's giving him pound.

"Oh, so Pierre told us he's bringing crepes. Kiko thought she was on a roll and tried to clown Pierre: 'I bet they're scrummy too!'

"Nobody laughed; they just ignored Kiko. She tried to copy Tony, but as usual she was a day late and a dollar short, trying to come up on her jokes, but her timing was off. Anyways, I suggested we shoot hoops, boys against the girls.

Fola said, "Let's do it,' and errbody was down wit' it. How fast can you get over here? We're 'bout to play, and I want you on my team."

Holding the phone closer to my face, I question, "Thought you said boys against the girls?"

"I did. We don't have enough girls, so I want you on my team. Jose and Tony are on the soccer field, kicking the ball around. I'ma ask them to play too."

"Um, I'm not feelin' it."

"Aw, come on, Kyndle. Forget about what those fools think. Don't let them steal your joy. Today begins our break and we should be celebrating; besides I need you."

Giving in, I agree, "Okay, I have to stop by my locker first, then I'll meet you over there."

Satisfied Tinah says, "Cool."

I put my phone inside my pocket, and start walking towards my locker in B hall. Turning the corner, I see Markie standing in front of his locker. He immediately nods and starts coming towards me. "What did Miss Fatona say?"

"Man, I was worried she was going to be mad that I didn't answer her question, but she wasn't. She told me not to worry, and that was that."

"I know you're glad that's over; looks like you were sweating bullets."

"No lie. I was trippin'. It was freakin embarrassing. But I'ma prove to everybody I'm still on top of my game, watch! My speech will be fire. I'm heading to shoot some hoops with Tinah 'n' em. Want to come?"

"Bet." Markie's in.

My cell phone starts buzzing, It's Tinah again!
"WYA"

I text back, "OMW."

As Markie and I get closer, Tinah cups her hands around her mouth, yelling, "Hurry up!"

We join the group and can see Tinah's head moving like she's jammin' to music as she tells Fola, "Since we don't have enough girls, I got Kyndle, and you can have Markie."

I'm surprised they're just now discussing teams.

Fola, being no pushover, responds, "Hold up, Ms. Bossy. We all know Kyndle can hoop; why should you automatically get to choose him?"

"'Cause I'm the one who asked him to play."

Standing there as though this little spat isn't about me, I keep my mouth shut because I could care less. Truth is, I only agreed to play because Tinah begged me to. As far as I'm concerned, Fola is boosie anyway.

Kiko interrupts the brewing spat. "Why don't you guys flip for them?"

Scrolling through Instagram posts, Maria nods her head, agreeing.

Without budging, Tinah continues making her case. "Fola, you should take Markie. I'm the reason Kyndle is here."

"You need to chill out, Tinah. It's not that serious. You act like we're in the NBA."

On that note, Tinah can't help it; she laughs because Fola is right.

Markie adds, "What makes you think I want to be on Fola's team, Tinah? You should have asked me first."

Immediately Tinah gets defensive. "Um, I didn't even know you were comin' to play."

I interject, "I invited him."

Tinah chills. "You're right, Markie. Do you want to be on my team or Fola's?"

"I really don't care whose team I'm on; it's the principle. You feel me?"

"I feel you. My bad," Tinah apologizes.

Maria finally looks up from her cell to interrupt the squabble. "Who has a coin? Heads, we get Kyndle; tails, Markie is with us."

Tinah agrees. "That's what's up, as long as Fola doesn't flip the coin. It's good!"

As Tony reaches into his pocket for a coin, Markie states, "I got skillz too, so whoever gets me is lucky. Y'all better recognize."

"No dis, Markie. It's just that I had already asked Kyndle." Tinah must be feeling some kind of way.

Markie tells Tinah, "Let's move on. It's good."

Tony holds up the quarter asking, "Who's going to flip it?"

Simultaneously, Tinah and Fola say, "Jose. Oh, snap!" They smile.

Placing his foot firmly on top of the bright-lime-colored ball, Jose gets the coin from Tony. Then he rubs the coin between his thumb and index fingers as everyone circles around him watching. He tosses the coin up high into the air. It somersaults, doing flips before hitting the ground hard and rolling a few feet away.

We follow the coin to the spot where it lands on heads.

Elated, Tinah says, "Kyndle, come wit' us."

She gathers her team and begins whispering a plan of attack.

Tinah directs me, "When you jump for the ball, make sure you hit it in Kiko's direction. I'll be waiting down court near the hoop. Maria, you block Markie."

Meanwhile Fola's team crowds around him, listening to instructions. "Markie, when the ball goes up, jump as high as you can and tip it over to Krishna."

"No problem," Markie says confidently.

Pierre takes the ball from Fola. "I'll toss it."

Markie and I stand so close that each of our breaths warms the other's face.

Pierre tosses the ball up high. Markie stretches his arm high into the air; and, with a wide-open hand he slaps it hard.

Dang, how did I let that happen? I think as my teammates yell, "Get the ball, Kyndle!"

Running as fast as I can to get the rebound before Krishna does, I am surprised when Maria gets it and tosses it to Kiko. Kiko passes it to me. I throw it down court to Tinah. She goes for a layup. The ball is in midair when Pierre smacks it away from the hoop. Fola rebounds and scores the first two points, then he comes for me. "Can you answer that, Kyndle?"

I am thinking, *What? Fola's punking me?* So I respond, "What did you say?"

He repeats himself. "I said, answer that! Since you couldn't answer Miss Fatona's question, maybe you have an answer to my two points in your face."

At that moment I want to charge Fola like a bull chasing a matador, but I think about what my parents always say: "Don't let anybody sucker you into acting stupid. Dignity always wins over stupidity. Like Michelle Obama said, 'When they go low, we go high.'"

If looks could kill, Fola would be dead. I don't need to say anything to him. What I need to do is out-think him. Get the ball and hurry up and score so I don't have to hear his mouth. He doesn't realize how much this is motivating me to outscore him.

The loud bell chimes from the clock tower: ding, ping, ding, ping, ding-ding, ding, ping. It is four o'clock. Looking up, I can see my mom's car crawling into the school parking lot.

I forgot she's taking me to the barber to get cut today.

"I'm outta here. Catch y'all week after next."

The girls all say, "Bye, Kyndle."

"Rematch when we get back from break," Fola shouts.

I reply "Bet."

I tell Markie, "Check you later."

3

Trick Question?
Today, the weekend begins

A HEAPING PILE OF backpacks lies on the court bench. I find mine buried beneath Fola's blue and gold Golden State Warriors backpack. Tossing his aside, I grab my red and gold 49er backpack, and place the wide cushy strap over my shoulder. Next, I jog towards Mom's army-green Jeep Grand Cherokee. She's standing next to the driver's side door, talking to a parent, when I approach and say, "Hi."

"Hi, Son."

The lady replies, "Hi."

Mom finally finishes talking. She hops in and straps on her seatbelt. I do the same before we take off. Looking at me she remarks, "You look dismal. How was your day?"

"Okay."

Not convinced, she forcefully says, "You're slouching, are you okay?'

"I'm all right."

"Well, you don't look all right, sitting there slouched in your seat. Sit up!"

I straighten up.

"What's going on?"

"Nothing much."

"Are you sure? You're acting strange for someone who gets a week off from school. Seems to me that you'd be acting more alive. Instead you're sitting there like today is the end of the world. What happened?"

"Nothing really. Same ol' thing."

Eyeing me, she doesn't buy it. Rapidly she fires off questions.

"How was math?"

"It was cool. We had a quiz today, and I aced it."

"And science?"

"All good. We're still studying DNA."

"Did you get any of your homework completed?"

"No. It's break. No homework."

"Did you turn in the permission slip?"

"Mmm-hmm."

Annoyed, my mother says, "What's with you? Speak to me with words and quit acting like a two-year-old."

"Yeah, I turned in my permission slip."

"'Yeah.' How about yes? That's good; you did what you were supposed to do, so what's the problem? Did Miss Fatona ask what Soul food dish you're bringing?"

"No, but she did ask for the origin of the food."

"Hmmp. Interesting question. What did you say?"

IDK!

"I couldn't give an answer, so I ended up looking like a fool, sitting in my seat, dumbfounded. Everyone who turned in their permission slips answered her question except me and Tinah! Tinah wasn't allowed to answer because she didn't turn in her permission slip. She said her mother is not feeling well and she's emailing hers later."

"I see."

With frustration, I blurt, "Kiko is Japanese, and her food comes from Japan. Krishna is Indian. He's bringing Indian food. Jose is Mexican; he's bringing Mexican food. Fola is Nigerian. He's bringing Nigerian food......... The whole class named the origin of their food. I'm Black. I'm American. My food is not called Black American food. We call it Soul food. Miss Fatona asked me to stay after class to talk about my assignment. She was surprised that I couldn't answer her question and wanted to know what was up. I told her I wasn't prepared because I didn't know it was part of our assignment. That's when she told me not to worry, but to make sure I include the food origin in my paper."

Mom places her free hand on my shoulder to console me. "Don't worry; you got this. The history of our food is complicated. You'll know the answer to Miss Fatona's question in time for your presentation. I'm sure your dad and grandparents will help too. Sometimes it takes a village."

Too consumed with the earlier events of the day, I think, *Wonder who came up with the name "Soul food" anyway? The name doesn't give a clue about where it's from, and it doesn't sound like it's American. There's Chinese American, Mexican American, and Italian American food. What happened to Black American food?"*

Snapping back into reality, I focus on what Mom is saying and ask, "What village?"

"We'll talk about that later!"

While heading to the barbershop, we keep talking, and I tell her about how uncomfortable I was when Miss Fatona asked the question. "It felt like a trick question."

With compassion Mom says, "I can imagine how awkward that was for you."

"I could hear giggling behind my back. Maria asked, 'Is Soul food from Seoul, Korea?' I don't know why she decided to play me. Tinah had my back though. She told Maria, 'Quit acting stupid,' but got into trouble for it. Miss Fatona sternly put Tinah in check. I felt bad for her. Krishna asked if 'Soul' is spelled the same as Seoul in Korea. He was outta pocket. He was piggybacking off Maria's question. I sat in my seat, getting madder by the minute. Rather than laughing at me like everyone else, Tinah could feel my pain. The whole situation was outta pocket. Humiliating!"

Sitting in the car with my fresh cut, after talking to Mom, I feel much better. Time to head home.

She parks her Jeep next to Dad's old-school forest-green Mercedes. Once inside, we go to Mom's room, and find Dad streaming his favorite episode of *Greenleaf*. Mom greets Dad with a peck on the cheek, then he asks, "How was your day?"

Removing her shoes and jacket, she responds, "Good. How was yours?"

While they do their routine chitchat, I sit opposite Dad in an old looking antique type chair at the foot of their bed.

They finish talking, and Dad says to me, "You're not too grown to give me a hug are you?"

I'm thinking, *Yes*. I love my dad, but I'm not a little boy anymore. I'm almost a teenager. His hug typically is followed by him rubbing my head and claiming it. I've outgrown this ritual of ours.

Reluctantly I stand, chuckle awkwardly, and step toward Dad to give him a hug. He places his hand atop my head, asking, "How's my head doing today?"

I give the expected answer: "Okay."

My dad calls my head his head because he helped create my head. He once told me that his mom did the same thing to him, so I guess I'm doomed. He's showing affection, but I'm getting too old for it. When I was younger, it was cool, but he doesn't realize that I am so over it. I wish he would stop it, but I don't want to hurt his feelings, so I must figure out a way to let him know I don't like it, and it isn't fun or funny anymore.

"What kind of answer is that? You don't sound like a Bendle. How was school?"

Jumping in, Mom answers for me, "All the kids in Kyndle's history class answered a question that he couldn't. We need to do a better job of teaching him about our cultural food and history."

"Ella, you didn't give him a chance to answer. And I have no idea what you are talking about!"

"I'm sorry; it's just that I'm frustrated too. It's really not his fault that he couldn't answer the question. Especially since there's no easy answer. Kyndle, tell your dad what happened."

I explain, "I was the only person in my history class who couldn't state the origin of the food I'm sharing."

"Slow down. What food?"

"Oh sorry, our International Day program is week after next."

"What's International Day?"

"It happens every year. This year my history class was selected to plan the program. We basically celebrate diversity and cultural differences. Last year's celebration was headed by Miss G.'s class."

"Who is Miss G.?"

"Miss Granberry is the resource coordinator for math at our school. Anyway, last year they had different dance troupes—African, Mexican, and Japanese—poetry readings, a sumo wrestling demonstration, and face painters. It was cool! This year our class is in charge of the program. We're having a cultural feast, and everybody is bringing their cultural food to share. I have to give a speech about my cultural food and its origin."

Now that Dad has the background information, he says, "So what happened?"

"I couldn't state the origin of my cultural food."

"That is an interesting question." Dad ponders, "Where does Soul food come from? Let me think about it. How to explain this? It may take a village to answer this one."

Thinking about the mouthwatering food makes me salivate. I love my mom's perfectly seasoned, crispy, golden-brown fried chicken—crunchy outside and juicy inside. My dad's collard greens, superbly textured. My granny's okra and tomatoes with Grandad's hot water cornbread and crunchy seasoned fried catfish. Granny's peach cobbler for dessert with a scoop of homestyle vanilla ice cream. Mmm, mmm, mmm. I am getting hungry just thinking about it.

When I reflect on how my classmates' choices are linked to their ancestry, I feel cheated. I chose food from my ancestry too! I

IDK!

am Native Black American. My lineage is African; I'm not! And I am bringing Soul food dishes. It sounds crazy!

I have a week to gather more information for my report and speech. I'm no sucka, and there is no way I am going to let Maria or anyone else in my class think I'm stupid. They will wish they had never clowned me after hearing my speech.

4

Win By Two
Friday Night

THE EPISODE OF Greenleaf ends after Grace tells her family she has a son. I head downstairs to the family room to use my Playstation, and play Among Us on the big-screen TV. The spaceship is full of astronauts, and I'm tryin' to figure out who is fake. Just as I'm about to take a shot, my dad yells from the top of the stairs, "Let me beat you one on one?" Distracted, I misfire and lose. Game over!

I yell back, "Okay."

In my room, I change into my Nike basketball shorts and my number 24 Bryant jersey in honor of my favorite player Kobe, who tragically died in an airplane crash with his daughter and friends not so long ago. I still can't believe he's gone. Thinking about Kobe makes me sad, and I've had enough misery for one day. First, I couldn't answer Miss Fatona's question; next Fola made his shot before me in our basketball game, and then some girl in New Jersey calling herself Bessie Coleman beat me in *Among Us*.

Can this day get any worse?

Dad seems pumped when I join him in the backyard. He asks, "Do you want to play best of seven, eleven, or twenty-one?"

"How much do you want to lose by?"

Dad can't contain himself; he laughs heartily at my challenge.

Hooping is one of the things Dad and I enjoy doing together. I really want to win this game, because I need something to go right for me today. "Let's play for eleven. Win by two."

The rules are set; I take the ball behind the top of the key and check it. Smoothly moving past my dad for a layup, I throw the ball so that it circles and spins around the rim before falling in. Now I'm on fire. Dad uses his body weight for defense, but I'm too quick for him. I snatch the ball and make an and-one.

Dad doesn't miss the opportunity to talk smack. "Anybody can do a layup; take the long shot. That crossover was weak. A pro wouldn't take that shot!" Dad keeps talking trash while I run circles around him. The game is over in no time; I win with eleven to Dad's eight. I'm just that good! Dad's fist connects with mine, giving me props, before we head back inside to clean up our sweaty bodies before dinner.

To chill, I lay across my bed and stare at the queen. No, I'm not talking about Elizabeth. Beyonce! She's looking down at me from the poster taped to my ceiling. My mind wanders, and I think about the time Mom was disappointed when I told her I wanted to redecorate my room, and get rid of the Harry Potter theme. With excitement she suggested, "We should do a *Game of Thrones* theme."

"No, I have something else in mind. Can you take me to buy some posters?"

From the poster selection at Walmart, I chose Doja Cat, Ariana Grande, Rihanna and Queen B. Mom was astonished and seemed confused by my choices. She asked, "Why do you want these posters?"

I told her, *"Because they are fiiine!"* I'll never forget the look on her face.

Dad's booming voice calling from outside my bedroom door startles me. Hmm, I must've dozed off.

"Your mother says dinner will be ready in ten minutes."

Groggily I say, "Okay thanks," then quickly wash up and change from my basketball gear to a pair of Levi's and T-shirt.

Upon entering the kitchen, I hear my parents discussing my assignment. Enthusiastically, Mom tells me that she and Dad are looking forward to helping me because "It's long overdue for people in our country to learn about the history of our cuisine."

Bobbing his head in agreement Dad says, "Earlier you asked me to explain what I mean by 'it takes a village.' It is an old African proverb that means 'collective responsibility.' It is the responsibility of each one to teach one. When we all do our jobs collectively, we all share in the success. One can't become strong and smart without the help of others."

Mom adds to what Dad is saying. "That's right! Your village started with me and your dad, grandparents, aunts, and uncles. It grew to include neighbors and church members. When you began school, it expanded to include your teachers. Collectively everyone in your village takes responsibility for your success."

Dad affirms Mom's sentiments. "All of us can use a helping hand sometimes."

I'm starving, so I interrupt saying, "This is good stuff. Can we eat?"

She nods her head toward the pot on the stove. "You can fix your plate."

Dad and I load our plates with spaghetti. Before sitting, Mom places a large salad, and bottle of dressing on the table, then asks, "Can one of you take the bread out of the oven?"

"Sure!" Dad offers.

Instead of going to the oven to take the bread out, he starts making excuses for losing. "My game is off; I want a rematch." Next he changes the subject. "Who is a better player, LeBron or Curry?"

"You can't compare Curry to LeBron Dad. Curry is the best three-point-shooting point guard to ever play the game, and LeBron is the best power forward today. He can hold his own against any power forward."

"No way. Nobody could touch Magic. He played with style and finesse." Dad describes Magic's moves, a wide grin appearing across his face. "Magic knew how to entertain the crowd with his speed and control on the court. His crossover was smooth. No one could perform like Magic."

"Dad, Jordan beat Magic Johnson in the NBA Finals, and he has more rings. Curry is the best three-point shooter ever; LeBron is the best all-around player. He can guard, shoot, and dunk. Kobe is my favorite player for life, so I guess no one is the best."

"Don't dismiss Draymond and Kyrie. They are two powerhouses in their own right."

"You're right."

As if his fork is burning his fingers, he suddenly drops it, jumps up from the table, and quickly moves toward the oven. When he opens the oven door, a plume of smoke escapes. With crispy, black, burned edges, the bread appears ruined. Mom disappointedly shakes her head while looking at Dad.

"I'm sorry Ella, I forgot to take the bread out. I think it's salvageable. Another minute and we would have had to toss it."

Dad takes a butter knife and scrapes the edges to save the garlic bread. It works!

Bowing our heads silently, we give thanks before digging in. Chowing down on his spaghetti, Dad compliments Mom. "Mmm, this is good, Ella."

With my mouth full, I nod my head in agreement.

"Thank you. I made my sauce from scratch using fresh tomatoes."

Between bites Dad says, "To understand why our food is called 'Soul food,' you must understand the meanin' of 'Soul' for our people."

Mom has a slightly different point of view. "First you have to understand which foods were brought here from Africa."

Dad agrees. "Kyndle, I think your mother is right."

Mom continues, "Your dad is right too. This is not an easy topic. A lot needs to be researched. When our ancestors crossed the Middle Passage from Africa to the West Indies and the Americas, plants and seeds from Africa traveled aboard the ships with them."

Dad interjects, "Have you decided which foods you plan to share? Maybe we should start there."

"Good idea, Bendle."

My parents wait for my response. "How about our New Year's Day feast?"

Clearly my mother likes the idea.

"That's perfect!" she says excitedly. "We can make black-eyed peas, collard greens…"

"Hold on, Ella. This is Kyndle's project. We're here to help, not take over."

"Okay. Kyndle, what foods do you have in mind?"

"I was thinking about our traditional foods: black-eyed peas, cornbread, greens, ham, fried chicken and fish, sweet potato pie…"

"Boy, you've got to be kidding! That's a lot of food to buy and a ton of work. Besides, each dish needs to feed ten or more people. If your dad helps and your granny is willing to make her delicious sweet potato pies, I'm in. Maybe instead of fried chicken or catfish, we'll give them something different to try, like your dad's mouth-watering salmon croquettes. You can explain the cultural significance of the food, the origin, and why they are so important for us to eat at the beginning of each year."

We finish eating, and Mom commands, "You guys have kitchen duty."

Dad tries to get out of cleaning by suggesting we flip a coin. "Heads or tails?"

Before he flips it, Mom cautions, "Kyndle, you should flip. Your dad has a tricky way of flipping, and he usually wins."

Pretending to be offended, Dad responds, "I would not cheat him."

To demonstrate he has no tricks, Dad tosses the coin up, and it lands on heads near the refrigerator on the kitchen floor.

Still leery, my mother urges, "Bendle, let Kyndle flip it."

"It's okay, Dad can flip it."

"You want heads or tails?"

"Heads."

Dad tosses the coin up again. Hitting the floor, it spins like a spinning top before landing on heads. Mom's elated, as though she has won a bet. Her broad smile quickly turns to a frown when Dad heads to his chair instead of the kitchen sink.

Frustrated, she says, "Just forget it! I'll do the dishes myself."

Dad sits and flips through channels, calling out to Mom, "Ella, you don't have to clean the kitchen. I got it."

Since his words don't match his actions, Mom ignores him and begrudgingly starts busting suds. She tells me to clean the counters, sweep, and take out the trash. After the kitchen is clean, I say good night to Dad. Mom doesn't utter a word to him; we both head upstairs to our bedrooms.

5

WHAT IS SOUL FOOD
Saturday Morning

LAST NIGHT MOM reminded me that my spring break doesn't mean a break from doing my weekend chores. I wake up early, like it's any other school day, except my house is silent; the sounds I hear, are my own. Deciding to get my chores out of the way before doing research, I find a bucket, broom, mop, rags, and cleaning supplies in the garage.

Now the stairs are gleaming, the porch is swept, and the Pine-Sol smell lingers in the sparkling clean bathroom. After showering, I put on my comfortable gray Nike sweatpants and black hoodie. Sitting on the edge of my bed, while putting on my Vans sneakers, I overhear my parents talking. Dad's explaining, "I told you I would clean the kitchen Ella, but before I got to it, you started. Remember!"

She responds, "You just sat there flipping channels."

"But that didn't mean I wasn't going to clean the kitchen. It would have gotten done, but you were impatient."

"You're right. I should have left the dishes for you! Oh well, let's move on."

Dad says, "Not before I get a hug?"

I can't see them, but I'm assuming they hugged before I hear their bedroom door open and footsteps marching downstairs.

I do the same after tying my shoes. Mom is in the kitchen filling her water bottle. She greets me, then says, "I'm about to head out to go hike Pena Adobe."

"Who's all going?"

"Let's see." Counting on her fingers, she names, "Jaylynn, Sonya, Celestine, Jasmir, Michelle, Myila and Stacey. They're in.

"What about Ms. Camille, and ……"

Before I finish my sentence Mom adds, "Christell, Audrey, Sharon and Charlette are not coming."

"They flaked?"

"No, they have other plans."

"That's flaking!"

Mom chuckles, "I better get going. I'm supposed to be there in thirty minutes, and I don't want to be the one holding everybody up. See you later."

"Okay."

Sitting at the kitchen table, I power on my MacBook, open Google, and search "What is Soul food?" The first thing that pops up is Wikipedia: "Soul food is a variety of cuisine popular in

African American culture. It is closely related to the cuisine of the southern United States." This is exactly what I was hoping to find.

Next, I google, "What were favorite foods of Black people in the 1800s?"

- *Collard greens, potato salad, peach cobbler, pound cake, fried catfish, cornbread, lemonade, hush puppies, hoppin' John, and chicken shortcake.*
- *When enslaved Black people escaped to freedom from Southern states to Northern states, they took many of their Southern cooking traditions with them.*
- *When Africans were brought to the United States as enslaved people, they brought okra, sesame seeds, peanuts, black-eyed peas, and rice. Using these foods along with the small portion of rationed foods like cornmeal and pork, given to them weekly, Africans introduced new recipes to American households.*
- *From the time of George Washington, the first president of the United States, several African American chefs have run the White House kitchen.*
- *Plantation owners sometimes allowed enslaved people to have small vegetable gardens. The vegetables they grew, like collard greens, added much-needed nutrients to their diets. They called the seasoned water that the vegetables were cooked in pot liquor (or pot likker). Slave families dunked cornbread into the pot likker so no nutrients were wasted.*

- *The black-eyed pea is a light-brown pea with a small black dot on it. These peas from West Africa were brought to America in the 1600s during the slave trade.*
- *The practice of eating black-eyed peas for luck is generally believed to date back to the Civil War. These peas were a food staple for slaves.*
- *Okra and gumbo are both words originating from Africa.*
- *Okra and watermelon originate from Africa.*
- *The consumption of chitlins (hog intestines) dates to slavery, when most slaves were given one week off between Christmas and New Year's. During that time slaveholders gave the slaves gifts of hand-me-down items and scraps of food they didn't want, all of which found its way into Soul food.*

I've heard my grandad say, "One man's trash is another man's treasure." Now I totally get it. Food given to slaves is a perfect example; the scraps the slaveholders considered unworthy for their consumption became enslaved Africans treasure. Foods high in protein, vitamins, and fiber helped them survive.

As I continue jotting down notes on 3x5 cards, the front door opens. The pitter-patter of Charkoal's paws against the wood floor gets louder as she trots into the kitchen. Mom's soft-sole hiking boots barely make a sound when she enters behind Charkoal. Looking up from my computer, I ask, "How was your hike, Ma?"

"It was good. We ran into Jennie's Outdoor Diva's and ended up walking with them on some trails I haven't been on before."

Charkoal walks over and stands on her hind legs, placing her paws firmly on my lap, begging for some love. I oblige by giving her a good rub.

Noticing the scattered note cards on the table, Mom saunters over, picks one up, and starts reading. "I see you're taking care of business."

"I found some really good stuff about Soul food."

"See? I told you. You got this."

We both smile.

"Want some breakfast?"

"Sure. I can help."

"You sure?"

"I was about to take a break anyway."

While washing our hands, Mom instructs, "Get the mushrooms, onions, peppers, and eggs. Take the hot links out of the freezer. Let's start washing the potatoes."

We stand at the kitchen sink, rinsing potatoes and talking about Soul food. The job is done pretty quickly. While Mom pats the potatoes dry with a paper towel, I take the cutting boards from the drawer. Mom cuts potatoes into silver-dollar-size circles, then places them into the large stainless-steel bowl. Using just the right amount, Mom sprinkles Lawry's seasoning on the potatoes, adding black pepper, onions, and bell peppers before spooning the potatoes into the hot skillet that's coated with olive oil.

The kitchen door swings open, Dad enters, and Charkoal jumps from the couch, runs over to Dad and begs for attention.

"What the baby want? I know, you want a belly rub."

Mom hates it when Dad baby talks to Charkoal. "Lloyd Bendle, will you stop all that babbling?"

Doesn't stop him, though. Dad makes his way to his favorite chair, sits down, and allows Charkoal to jump onto his lap while he rubs her belly.

"How the baby doin'? Hmm, Charkoal?"

Dad tires of rubbing Charkoal. "Okay, that's enough. Get down."

Charkoal ignores him. She begs for more. Dad gives in and rubs her more.

After a while he tires and uses his commanding voice this time. "Get down now, Charkoal."

The sound of Dad's gruff voice alarms her; she jumps from his lap and scurries back to her spot on the couch.

Mom comments, "Bendle, you baby her too much. You give her an inch, and she takes a mile."

Dad grins, knowing Mom is telling the truth. Switching the subject, he asks, "What can I do to help?"

"Can you help Kyndle with the eggs?"

"I'm on it!"

"Breakfast wouldn't be the same without my gourmet eggs." He compliments himself.

Adding butter to the large skillet, Dad sautés all the veggies. I crack nine eggs without getting any shells in the bowl. After the eggs are thoroughly mixed, Dad says, "Kyndle, hand me the eggs."

He pours the scrambled eggs into the sautéed veggies and gently folds everything together until they're moist and fluffy.

I take my job of cooking biscuits seriously, placing each biscuit about two fingers apart on the cookie sheet before placing them into the oven. Finally everything is done and ready to eat. The dirty dishes are placed in the sink filled with hot, soapy water.

The food smells so good that I want to dig in right away. But before we do, my father directs, "Kyndle, say grace."

With closed eyes and a bowed head, I begin, "Heavenly Father, thank you for this day. Thank you for the food that nourishes our bodies. Thank you for the hands that prepared this meal, and I pray for my grandparents, cousins, friends, and those who are less fortunate. Amen!"

Dad pays his usual compliment: "Good job."

We finally dig in. The eggs are fluffy, the biscuits are golden, the potatoes are moist and well-seasoned, and the meats are cooked to perfection. Stuffed, none of us feel like cleaning, but it has to be done. When Mom starts clearing the table, Dad says, "I got this, Ella."

Mom finishes placing dishes in the sink and retreats to her bedroom. I start to help, but Dad says, "I got this, relax." So, I follow Mom's lead and go to my room to chill.

After learning so much about the origin of some of the foods we eat, I make up my mind to check in with Fola on a few things. We haven't really talked since he tried to front me on the court. Now that I've learned so much about my cultural food, I decide to be the bigger person and reach out.

 'Hey Cuz'

What up Cuz? You the last person I thought I'd hear from. LMAO

 Lol! It's a new day Cousin.

 "That's what's up! My bad for dissing you on the court. I was in my feelings and was just joshing you."

 It's good, just don't do it again. Let me hit you live.

 K

We stop texting, and I call Fola.

He picks up asking, "What you doin'?"

"Just finished eating breakfast. Before that, I was doin' research for our assignment. Getting it in before we leave for our vacation. Question for you: Does your mother cook with okra, black-eyed peas, or collard greens?"

"Yep, all that. My mom cooks red red, African stewed black-eyed peas, all the time. She puts collard greens in my favorite dishes, *egusi* and *fufu*. I think she'll make it for International Day. You might get to try it."

"Is anything else in egusi?"

"It's made with different meats, ground pumpkin seeds, melon seeds, and okra to make it thick and creamy. Sometimes she makes it with pumpkin leaves when she can find them, but mostly she uses collards."

"Cool man, this is exactly what I needed to know."

"Wait, wait, you didn't tell me why you need to know?"

IDK!

"My bad. No biggie. I'm comparing foods we eat today that originated in Africa. That's all. You'll get the whole scoop when I give my speech."

"Bet."

"Okay cool, check you layta."

"Layta."

We both hang up.

My phone buzzes again, it's Fola texting.

 "Sorry for speaking on you earlier, it wasn't cool."

 I reply, "NP. We straight."

My mom starts calling my name. "Kyndle."

I call out, "Ma, did you call me?"

"Yes. Maria is on the phone."

"Okay." I go to my parent's room to pick up the landline. "Hello?"

"Hi, Kyndle."

"Hi, Maria. How did you get this number?"

"My mother got it from the school directory."

"Oookay. What's up?"

"I'm taking a break from working on my project and decided to give you a call."

"Oookay. What's up?"

"So anyway, what are your plans during break?"

Despite her being so nosy, I answer her question.

"I'm going to Markie's later today and Monday we leave for So Cal."

"What are you going to do down there?"

"Visit my cousin and uncle."

"What's happening at Markie's?"

It feels like Maria's grilling me, so, I'm going to end this convo.

"Maria, I better get off the phone; we're about to leave."

"Okay, Kyndle. Guess I'll talk to you later."

"Sounds good! Bye, Maria."

"Bye, Kyndle."

That girl is always pressed to talk!

6

MANNY VS MONEY
Saturday Afternoon

FINALLY I'M RINGING Markie's doorbell. His mother opens the door. "Hi, Kyndle. Come in."

"Hi, Mrs. Ramos."

As I greet her, she yells, "Marcos, Kyndle is here!"

Markie's family calls him by his government name, Marcos. He's named after his grandfather on his dad's side, who lives in the Philippines. Markie comes out of his room. We pound, bumping our fists. I look to my right, where Mr. Ramos and Markie's Uncle Ry are sitting on a worn army-green couch, streaming ESPN re-runs of Manny Pacquiao versus Floyd "Money" Mayweather. They are both yelling at the flat-screen TV mounted on the wall in front of them. You would think that the game was streaming live.

"Move faster! Swing left, duck, duck, move, move!"

Manny Pacquiao can't hear their instructions, but I'll bet the neighbors can.

"If he had moved faster, he could have beat Money," Mr. Ramos excitedly screams. Markie told me his dad's favorite fighter is Pacquiao because he's from the Philippines.

Mrs. Ramos and Mr. Ry's girlfriend bring in food from the kitchen. Mrs. Ramos's homemade quesadillas, salsa, and nachos look so good. Her family came from Mexico, so she really knows how to hook up some good Mexican food.

She asks, "Kyndle, are you hungry?"

"No, thank you."

"Well, you need to taste some of this good food. Just a little bit, okay?"

Even though I'm still full from breakfast, I don't resist. The food looks tasty, and I know it will taste as good as it looks, so I accept.

"Marcos, you and Kyndle go fix your plates."

Markie and I go directly into the kitchen, grab plates, and fill them with nachos: shredded beef, lots of melted cheese, jalapeños, and freshly made salsa. Next, we go to Markie's room to watch ESPN reruns of the eleventh and twelfth rounds. We already know the outcome, but I enjoy watching Floyd win by unanimous decision.

Markie's family loves boxing. Last year I took lessons with Markie. He's been taking boxing lessons since he was in the third grade and says he plans to become a professional. As his friend, I feel it's my duty to talk him out of it. My dad says only a few people make it to become professional athletes. That's why I'm not banking on becoming a basketball star. Markie's pretty smart, so he should shoot for some other profession—maybe science since he likes making hypotheses and doing experiments.

I brought my Oculus headset with me, so Markie and I could play Vader Immortal. After he wins, we switch from the Oculus to hooping in his backyard. I rule on his court, so he suggests, "Man, let's play one more game?"

After he loses again, I give him another chance to redeem himself.

"Okay, let's make this the last game."

After I win again, Markie raises his voice, shouting, "I'm done."

"No problem man, you good?"

I think he realizes he is being ridiculous because he calmly says, "Yeah, let's go inside."

We head back into the house and make a beeline for the kitchen to get more food. We both load our plates and dig in. As I'm gulping down the last of the horchata, my cell phone begins buzzing.

 It's my mother. Her text says, "We're outside."

I type, "Okay. Be right out."

Mom replies, "Remember to thank the Ramos' for their hospitality. Oh, and tell Leti I'll call her later to discuss the PTA meeting. Don't forget."

 I text, "K" then send.

I thank Mrs. Ramos for the delicious grub and tell her, "My mother says she'll call you later."

Next, I say goodbye to Mr. Ramos and Mr. Ry, who are still talking about the fight. Markie walks with me to the car to greet my parents before we leave.

When I hop in the back seat, my dad asks, "How was your visit?"

"It was good. I'm stuffed. Mrs. Ramos cooked a bunch of food."

"Oh yeah, what did she cook?"

"Nachos with shredded beef, cheese quesadillas, and chicken enchiladas."

Mom states, "I can't believe you ate all that food after that big breakfast we had."

"I wasn't going to, but Mrs. Ramos insisted I eat something, and it looked so good I couldn't help myself, I had to try some! How was the movie?"

Mom answers first. "Your dad picked the movie. It was too much cussing and shooting for me. I don't know how it got its PG-13 rating. My eyes were closed more than they were open."

Dad adds, "Well, I guess your mother is right. I don't know how *F9: The Fast Saga* is rated PG-13, but I do know it's a good movie." Winking, he adds, "Your mother gets to pick the next movie. Sounds like you and Markie had a nice time. What else did you do besides eat?"

"We shot hoops and played Oculus games. Markie beat me in Oculus, and I ruled on the court. He got a little mad when I kept winning the basketball games, but he got over it."

"Well, I'm glad Markie wasn't irritated for too long," Mom adds.

7

GRANDAD SAYS
Saturday Night

It always seems like it takes longer to get to Markie's house than it does to get back home. As soon as we walk through the front door, Dad enthusiastically announces, "Doc Claylea is the guest preacher tomorrow at Sojourner. That man can preach, and I want to be on time!

We say good night and head to our bedrooms.

After service tomorrow, we'll have dinner with my grandparents. Monday, we leave for So Cal. My grandparents' church tends to go on and on, taking what feels like forever, especially during revival or when there is a guest preacher. Rev. Dr. Claylea is a friend of Rev. Kamal's, and seems to get invited to preach whenever Rev. Kamal is out of town. Technically, my grandparents church is my dad's church, but he only goes on special occasions.

When I go to church with my mother, we usually get out within an hour, and she doesn't care what I wear.

At St. Benedicts the choir doesn't wear robes like they do at my grandparents' church. The singing is as good as it is at Sojourner, but there's a lot of standing up and sitting down, which I could do without. Father Jay and Jayson read the same prayers year after year from the Roman Missal, held by an altar boy or girl. Passing the sign of peace is my favorite part of service, when we greet one another, "Peace be with you." That's when the priests walk down the aisle, greeting everyone. My family hugs each other before passing peace to others. It's the time during the service that the church feels like family. Both priests are funny, always making the congregation laugh during the homily. Father Jay uses his smooth, melodic voice to relate the religious topic to our daily lives and Father Jayson usually relates the homily to a personal experience.

Nothing at St. Benedicts seems unplanned. It's very orderly, and if it were not for the vibrant personalities of Fr. Jay and Jayson, it could be boring. We recite the same prayers and profession of faith every Sunday. The service usually ends in about an hour unless a baptism causes the service to last longer.

At my grandparents' church, Sojourner Truth Pentecostal, prayers are not read from a book. Rev. Dr. Claylea relates the topic to our lives too; he just uses a longer route to get to the point. With his head bowed and eyes closed, Dr. Claylea says what the Lord tells him to say. The sermon is not read; No matter whose preaching, words are usually coming from the heart.

Since my dad is old school, he forces me to wear a blazer when we go to Sojourner. Not so long ago, my mom convinced him that it was okay for me to wear jeans instead of slacks. I think my dad finally got it, after seeing Rev. Claylea wearing jeans in the pulpit.

The funny thing is, both churches preach the same message: Love God, love one another, and help your fellow man.

Just before I get in bed, I lay out a clean t-shirt, and blazer. I can't decide between my Purple or Levi's jeans, so I lay both pairs at the foot of my bed and will decide in the morning.

Every night my mother gets on her knees and says her prayers. She continues to tell me that I should do the same. Seems to me I should be able to pray in any position. I do say my prayers almost every night. The difference is, I say them while I'm lying down. Instead of looking at my posters, I close my eyes. I think God can still hear me.

"Dear God, Heavenly Father, Almighty, thank you for this day. Thank you for the delicious food I ate today—the delicious breakfast my family prepared and Mrs. Ramos's food. Bless my grandparents, my parents, my friends, my cousins, aunts, and those who are less fortunate. These blessings I asks for in the name of the Father, Son, and Holy Spirit."

Sunday Morning

I awaken to the sound of drawers opening and closing. Somebody is up getting ready for church.

When I enter the kitchen, I find Dad standing in front of the open refrigerator, staring inside. I greet him, "Good morning."

Still peering inside the fridge, he says, "Good morning," and grumbles, "There's nothing in here to eat. Guess I'll have an English muffin."

He closes the fridge and opens the bread box that sits on the counter. "Want one?"

"Sure."

Just as the toasted muffins pop up, Mom pops in wearing black and white from head to toe.

"Ella, Kyndle and I settled on eating muffins for breakfast; doesn't look like we have much else to choose from."

"I don't know what you are talking about. We have all kinds of food: fresh fruit, eggs, grits, cereal, yogurt, and you still have that ham you bought in the freezer. Seems to me you just didn't look, Bendle."

"That's because the refrigerator needs to be organized. There's too much in it, and I don't feel like hunting for food."

"Sounds like a personal problem to me. Guess it's time for you to clean and organize it then. Besides, a grown man can fend for himself and prepare what he wants to eat."

Moving on from her dialogue with Dad, she says to me, "You look handsome."

"Thanks, Ma. I like your fit too."

Approaching Mom with outstretched arms, Dad hugs Mom stating, "My wife always looks gorgeous." He stands behind her, rubs her shoulders, then bends over and kisses her on the cheek as she puts a spoonful of cereal into her mouth. She finishes chewing and can't help but smile. Looks like she's already forgotten about Dad's refrigerator comment. My parents are funny, they seem to enjoy debating a lot, but it never seems to get too heated. Just friendly banter.

"Kyndle, I like your purple T-shirt; it looks nice with your blazer. Did you two coordinate intentionally?"

"No, we both really have good taste," Dad says with a smile.

As I'm chewing my buttery muffin, Mom's cereal is calling me. I scarf down the last bite of my muffin, swallow the last drop of orange juice, then get a bowl of cereal too.

Dad notices me getting a bowl and says, "I think I'll have some too."

We finish eating and place our bowls in the kitchen sink. There's no time for washing dishes now.

Before we leave Dad makes his usual request. "Kyndle, take a picture of me and your mom. Now, Ella, take a picture of me and Kyndle. Let me get you and your mom."

Using our cell phones, we snap a few more pics, and take a couple selfies, before heading out the door.

When we arrive at Sojourner Truth, the parking lot is full.

Dad remarks, "I knew we should have left a little earlier."

Mom urges, "Relax Bendle, we're not too late, the service is about to start.

"I know, but I want to get a good seat."

"Don't stress, we will!"

After parking on the street, we go inside and find seats a couple of pews behind my grandparents.

Mom was right as usual.

The choir is singing, "I'm Glad To Be In The Service One More Time." Just as two large monitors at the front left and right of the sanctuary light up with the words, Welcome Doctor Pastor Claylea, he approaches the pulpit.

Pastor Claylea stands before the congregation in a pair of white jeans, white sneakers, and a white graphic tee with these words printed in black, "God is good All the time!" His fit is nice!

Pastor begins, how great it is to be back in the house of the Lord with the Sojourner Truth family. After twenty-five minutes, he says, "I'm almost finished." Roughly forty-five minutes into his sermon, he says, "I won't be much longer." He keeps preaching. Ministers Tim White and Tony Adams stand and shout, "Yeah" urging the Pastor to keep saying what he's saying. Next, the deacons get on their feet to join the ministers, repeating "Yeah," with every word from Pastor Claylea's mouth.

Ministers Tim and Tony move closer to the Pastor as his sermon gradually crescendos to a high point. People fan themselves. Some jump up, shout or even run up to the front of the sanctuary when the Holy Spirit hits them. The sound of Pastor Claylea's baritone voice eases, the choir lifts their voices, and beautiful gospel songs amplify. The drum beat and majestic organ blares to replace Pastor Claylea's words. The congregation stands, hands clap, arms rise like reaching for heaven, folks turn to their neighbor and praise the Lord. Ushers dressed in black and white uniforms, pass Kleenex tissues to those who need to dry their eyes, from flowing tears of joy. God's presence can be felt, and folks know he will make a way. When it's time for the collection, Pastor reminds everyone of the ways they can give: "Download the Givelify app to your cell phone." Pointing to the right monitor, which now has a QR code on the screen and www.STPC.org.

Two ushers position themselves in front of the church just beneath the pulpit. They hold large white buckets to collect checks and cash donations. Some folks leave their seats to take up their offerings, while most remain seated using their cell phones. People cheerfully give while the choir sings; "You Can't Beat God Giving." On a high note, the soprano section end the song with .... no matter how you try. Within two hours the congregation is standing, singing the National Negro Anthem, "Lift Every Voice and Sing." After the benediction and closing prayer, Pastor Claylea says, "I want to thank my Mount Calvary Baptist Church members for giving me the opportunity to be here with you today. When you are in the Solano community, please come visit us there. A final amen is said by the entire congregation, then we are dismissed.

My parents and I wait in the narthex for my grandparents. Grandad approaches Dad with his hand extended. They shake vigorously.

Dad tells Grandad, "I really enjoyed the service. Doc had the church on fire.

Mom and Granny hug each other.

My grandad greets me. "You are a sight for sore eyes."

"Nice to see you too, Grandad."

Next I turn to give my grandmother a big hug and kiss on the cheek.

The adults spend another thirty minutes fellowshipping: Shaking hands, patting backs, smiling, and laughing. My grandparents have been members of Sojourner Truth Pentecostal for more than forty years. It seems like everybody knows them, and they know everybody. When Pastor Claylea finishes shaking hands with the Washingtons, my grandad approaches him.

He shakes the pastor's hand while telling him, "Doc, your sermon was inspiring."

We all follow suit, greeting Dr. Pastor Claylea before leaving church. My grandparents live just a few blocks up the hill from the church. As soon as we walk through the door, Mom and Granny take their shoes off, put on slippers, and find aprons in the kitchen. Dad and I take off our jackets. Grandad changes into something more comfortable.

Dad encourages me to talk to my grandad, "You should talk to Daddy about your project."

Grandad returns looking sharp and relaxed, wearing a Bricks & Wood jogging suit.

"I like your fit, Grandad."

"Thanks. I got it online from a Black-owned company."

"Cool." Looking at my dad, I say, "We need to check out the website."

He nods in agreement, then I redirect my attention to Granddad. "I have to prepare a speech about Soul food for an assignment, and I need some help with understanding why our food is named Soul food."

"If you need my help, Son, you got it!" He breaks into song. "Cause I'ma Soul man, I'ma Soul man, and Soul men like to eat Soul food." He chuckles before saying, "Seriously, though. This is a tough question. It might take a village to answer. You'll definitely want to get yo' granny's input too."

It's funny how everyone is saying it takes a village. Until this project I'd never heard this African proverb.

Grandad continues, "Now you know when you ask me a question, I'm gon' give it to you straight. Soul is important to our people 'cause it's somethin' that can't be taken away. It lives within us. We're born with it. It's not borrowed. It's our very own. We crowned singer James Brown, Soul Brother #1, and Aretha Franklin, Queen of Soul. Sam & Dave's song 'Soul Man' was a number one hit record. *Soul Train,* a popular dance show, gave *American Bandstand* a run for its money. Our musical genius created jazz, blues, rock and roll, rap, gospel, and R&B."

"Rock and roll?"

"Yes, look up Chuck Berry and Little Richard. If you wanted to find any of those genres back in my day, you looked in the Soul section at the record store."

I'm thinking, *Man, this was a long time ago. I've never been to a record store; my music is downloaded to my electronic devices, iPhone, iPad, and Mac.* As Grandad talks, I take it all in.

"The 5th Dimension sang 'Stone Soul Picnic.' If it was created by us, it was with Soul. Soul took on a new meaning for us. It meant pride. Pride in our cuisine, music, inventions and ourselves."

Grandad continues, "Our style of dress, dance, cooking, lingo, traditions are all the stuff that makes our culture unique. And don't get me started on all the inventions by Black folks that have contributed greatly to our country and the world. It's a shame that all Americans are not taught who John Lee Love is, the inventor of the pencil sharpener; Dr. Charles Drew, a pioneer in the field of blood transfusions; or Lewis Latimer, who found a way to make light bulbs last hours instead of minutes. Most Americans don't have a clue that the three-position traffic signal was invented by a Black man, Garrett Morgan. He sold the rights to his traffic signal to General Electric for forty thousand dollars.

That was a lot of money back then. He also invented a precursor to the modern gas mask. I'm not only thinkin' of men; the first self-made female millionaire in this country was a Black woman, Sarah Breedlove, better known as Madam C. J. Walker, inventor and manufacturer of hair care products. I could go on and on. Baby boy, if you didn't know, now you know. Look these entertainers and inventors up. Know your history. These Native Black Americans put their Souls into inventing things that continue to benefit humans worldwide."

Looking at me as though I am the only person in the room, Grandad says, "Don't ever believe that you don't have a culture or that others are more intelligent than you."

He closes his eyes while taking a deep breath. "Our people have fought against many atrocities. We fought for basic human rights, and today we continue trying to right wrongs. In the course of our struggles, we redefined the meaning of Soul. During the civil rights movement, we went from being called 'coloreds' to 'negroes,' then we named ourselves Black.

"Soul Brother No. 1, James Brown sang, 'Say it loud: I'm Black, and I'm proud.'" Grandad starts singing again, "Say it loud: I'm Black, and I'm proud. Say it loud: I'm Black, and I'm proud. One mo' time! Say it loud: I'm Black, and I'm proud."

Standing, Grandad can't help himself. He starts moving his big feet swiftly from left to right as he slides across the living room floor, singing, "Say it loud: I'm Black, and I'm proud."

The kitchen door swings open, and Granny and Mom rush into the living room to see what's happening. They join in as background singers. Every time Grandad says, "Say it loud," Dad, Granny, Mom, and I shout, "I'm Black, and I'm proud."

Grandad is old, but he still has it. His moves are on beat. Breathing heavily when he sits down, Grandad confesses, "Whew, I'm out of breath."

Mom admits, "Me too."

Singing with my family feels good. We actually harmonize pretty well. Mom has a pretty voice.

Grandad takes a deep breath before continuing. "Our history includes some very sad times. We suffered brutally for a long time. Unfortunately, oppressing our people was acceptable. Many of us feel the 1960s was a time when we made great progress. We protested peacefully with leaders like Dr. Martin Luther King, Rosa Parks, and Malcolm X. We fought against unfair Jim Crow laws, for our right to vote, and for equal employment opportunities; equal education; the right to use public facilities like restrooms, libraries, and restaurants; and the God-given right to be treated like any other human. Some progress was made, but new roadblocks continue to be placed in our way. We must continue to fight for what is right, fair and just. I know that sounds like it was a long time ago, but it wasn't. There's still plenty work to be done. Thank God for the young people who peacefully protest for Black lives, letting the world know that Black lives matter. It's really a shame that in this day and age, it's necessary to say we matter. We are still fighting, the good fight. We are strong people who persevere when confronted with hatred and adversity against us."

"That part!" Granny agrees.

I'm impressed with my granny. Look at her keeping up with the current slang.

Grandad concludes: "Our fight for equality benefits everybody, not only Black people. Whites, Asians, Latinos, all Americans. I thank God, you neva experienced hateful Jim Crow laws, and I pray to God you neva do. Because people fought for equality through peaceful protests, campaigns, and exercising their right to vote, positive changes continue to be made. Now, just because laws are made, doesn't mean they are fair. Oftentimes, people have to fight to make things right. Like civil rights activists did. Folks campaigned for over 10 years to get Dr. King's birthday to become a national holiday. After years, the anti-lynching law passed in 2022, and Juneteenth became a federal holiday in 2021. These accomplishments happened because people didn't give up. They fought the good fight! Remember our history is American history. In many ways, things are better than they used to be, but we still have lots of work to do."

When Grandad pauses, Dad takes the opportunity to yell toward the kitchen, "Is the food ready?"

Mom yells back, "Yes. You all can come help bring out the food and set the table."

Using the Notes app on my phone, I quickly type a few so I don't forget what my grandad said. Next I help set the table.

I've never seen my grandad get so emotional. He's so jovial and full of life; I didn't expect to see him get so serious when talking about our history. It's never a dull moment with him. His great sense of humor lightened up a somber subject. He can teach me any day!

After the table is set, we maintain our family tradition of holding hands and saying grace before eating.

Like my dad does to me, Grandad persuades him, "Lloyd will you say the blessing?"

Dad starts, "Dear Lord, thank you for this blessed day. Thank you for waking us up this morning. Thank you for giving us the strength to get to church this morning, to hear your words, oh Lord, and thank you for bringing my family together once again safely. We thank you for your continued blessings this day and every day. Amen."

Everyone says, "Amen."

The meatloaf, mashed potatoes and gravy, are on point as usual. They are my dad's favorites. The green beans, mac and cheese, and homemade buttery flaky biscuits, melt in our mouths. Granny never makes meatloaf without these sides. For dessert, Mom has picked up a peach cobbler from It's All Good Bakery in Oakland. There's way too much food. Granny prefers to have more than enough in case an unexpected guest drops in.

On the Sundays Granny cooks, she sends a plate to Miss Fannie, the next-door neighbor, and Mr. Jones, who lives around the corner. They are both seniors living alone. "Baby boy, now do you know how Soul food was named?" Granny asks.

"It makes a lot more sense to me now."

"Baby, Soul is from the heart. Soul can make you feel good. You see what it does to your grandfather."

Everyone bursts out laughing, including Grandad. "Black folks add a pinch of Soul to everything we create."

Granny asks, "Have you decided which dishes you're sharing?"

Before I answer, Mom butts in, "Kyndle wants traditional New Year's Day foods. I'm cooking black-eyed peas, okra and tomatoes, your recipe of course, greens, and cornbread. We're hoping you'll make sweet potato pies. Lloyd's making salmon croquettes. Kyndle will definitely share more about our traditional dishes in his presentation."

"Chil', that sounds good." Granny beams, showing her approval.

8

THE 1800'S
Sunday Night

Placing his hand on his belly as he reared back stretching, Grandad says, "Yo' grandmother's cooking is so good. It's a blessing to have a wife who can cook."

Dad nods in agreement.

Looking at Dad, Mom adds, "And a husband who can chop veggies and help clean."

Granny chuckles and nods in agreement with Mom.

While Dad and Grandad clear the table, I type more notes in my app with headings of "Introduction," "Body," or "Conclusion." When they return, Grandad continues, "The reason we eat black-eyed peas on New Year's Day is for good luck."

Dad adds, "Yeah, they taste good and are good for us. Black-eyed peas with okra are loaded with vitamin A and calcium. The next time we have black eyed peas, I'm going to use some leftovers and add to my smoothie. I can always use an extra boost.

Grandad is on a roll. "You see, in the early 1600s, captured African People were taken to Virginia and worked throughout the South. By the 1800s, Black folks was cookin' what White folks was eatin'. We were Southern cooks, creating American cuisine."

"But what about the people who were already here?"

With a sullen look on his face, my grandad explains, "Sadly, by the 1800s many Aboriginal Americans had been massacred. They were swindled out of their land and killed. When Christopher Columbus arrived in the late 1400s, there were roughly 15,000,000 Aboriginal American people living in North America. Don't just take my word for it; do your own research. By the late 1800s, there were fewer than 300,000 Aboriginal Americans left. What happened to them is another stain in our history that's glossed over.

Shaking his head Grandad says, "So back to why our food was what White folks was eatin'. We were their cooks. In 1865 the Thirteenth Amendment abolished slavery. A few years following the end of American slavery, Ellis Island opened to allow Europeans to immigrate here between 1892 and 1954. Over twelve million immigrants entered the United States. Many got a head start when they were given free land to ensure their success. The land was given under the Homestead Act, look it up. A few Black folks got some land too. But most of us are still waiting on our forty acres and a mule."

"Ump, forty acres and a mule huh?"

"It's another part of American history that doesn't get taught. It gets swept under the rug. Look it up. Bottom line is, at the end of slavery some free community leaders, mostly preachers, got together and worked out a deal to ensure former slaves received reparations. The plan was to redistribute 400,000 acres of southern coastal land to recently freed slaves. President Lincoln signed the order but, unfortunately after his assassination, President Andrew Jackson overturned it. He cared more about those who lost the civil war and returned the land back to them. When you hear folks saying they're waitin' for their forty acres and a mule, this is what they are talkin' 'bout. Other groups who have been wronged in this country, have received their reparations, and we're still waitin'. Anyway, back to what I was saying about us being the cooks who created an American cuisine. What I'm trying to explain is, we were doing a lot of cookin' in our country long before the new immigrants arrived. Immigrants introduced new types of foods too, but we had been cookin' on this here land for about 200 plus years before Ellis Island opened. Make sure you research our government's immigration policies of the late 1800s."

Granny interrupts, "Want to hear a true story that happened right here?" She dives in before anyone answers. Facing Grandad she says, "Fleming, do you remember when we hosted dinner for our Bible study group?"

"Uh-huh, I do!"

"Remember what what's-his-name said before we ate?"

"Who is what's-his-name?"

Looking frustrated, Granny says, "I'm trying to think of his name. My goodness, I can't think of their names to save my life."

"Ah, let's see. There was, oh, what's his name?" Grandad is thinking too, and then he remembers, "Johnny and Maria."

Hearing two of the names triggers Granny's memory.

"That's right!" Granny smiles. "Maria and John, Charlotte and Jorge—Easter Jean and Ruth Cook came together. The food was ready. Johnny said the blessing, and we fixed our plates, sat down, and began eating."

"'What is this?' Easter said after tasting my greens. 'It's delicious! Wow, it's so good! I've never tasted this before.'

"I answered, 'It's traditional Black Soul food.'

"Immediately, Johnny blurted out, 'It's not Black food; it's Southern cooking.'

"Naturally I responded: 'Who do you think was doing the cooking? The slaves.' Suddenly the room became so quiet that you could hear a mouse piss on cotton."

Boisterous, noisy laughter erupts as Granny tells her story. I imagine what a mouse pissing on cotton would sound like. By the time I get it, Their laughter died down.

Granny continues her story. "Of course, they seemed surprised. Guess I gave them somethin' to think about! Life is funny; the very foods that we've eaten traditionally for years have become so popular. Kale, collards, and mustard greens are all being called superfoods. Fried pork skin, once considered junk food, is now considered as a healthier choice to potato chips. The pork skins have lower carbs and higher protein. You can even get sweet potatoes in many restaurants today as an alternative to traditional baked potatoes or fries. The one constant in life is change. I guess if you live long enough, you'll get to see some things come full circle.

These days practically everybody from the South knows how to cook Soul food. I think that movie *The Help* really shed light on just how much Black folks taught White Southerners how to cook. Nowadays, it's called southern cuisine or comfort food. Our mothers taught folks from South to North how to prepare our delicious cuisine. It was one place where we had freedom to be creative."

"I sho do remember that day," Grandad chuckles. "I think Johnny turned beet red when you mentioned slaves cooking; guess he neva thought about it that way. But it was a nice evenin' with good friends, and everybody enjoyed yo' granny's cookin'. The meal was finished with yo' granny's delicious sweet potato pie. We were all stuffed and satisfied."

The lively discussion continues, and Granny adds, "That's right we had fun that evening, with good food and good wine, shared with good friends."

I break up the lively conversation asking, "Do you still meet for bible study with them?"

"No, after we moved and changed churches, we stopped meeting. I follow Johnny and Maria on Facebook though."

Dad interrupts, stating, "It's gettin' late, so we better get this show on the road. We have an early start tomorrow. Let's get the kitchen finished, or we'll be here all night."

Mom washes, Granny dries, I wipe the counters, Dad cleans the stove, and Grandad sweeps the floor. The kitchen is sparkling in no time. We hug each other before leaving. My grandparents watch us from their porch as we walk to the car. They wave, and Granny shouts, "Safe travels to Southern California. Be careful; there's always a fool on the road."

"We will. Love you!" Dad calls back.

On the drive home, Mom continues the discussion. "Kyndle, collard greens come from Africa too.

"I discovered that while doing my research online." I wonder why my family has never talked about the foods we eat like this before. I have a new appreciation for greens, yams, and black-eyed peas.

While listening to my parents on the ride home, I googled: Black people and collard greens history?

Here's what I found, "During the Middle Passage, these foods were introduced to America. Back in those days, Black people harvested some food for their families. Collard greens were one of the few vegetables that they were allowed to grow for themselves and their families. Even after the Native Black Americans were emancipated in the late 1800's, cooked greens were a comfort in the Black American culture."

I'm realizing, I don't know any Black people who don't eat cooked greens.

Still talking about the foods we eat, Mom states, "I like to mix my cooked greens with collards, mustards and a little bit of kale. Bendle, this is a good time to explain the significance of eating greens for the New Year," she advises.

"Before I do, I don't want to forget to say something else. Our ancestors were adept at preparing wild game. They fried, grilled, and roasted meats with the perfect seasonings to bring out the best flavors. Back then, people either fished or hunted for food."

Once Dad gets on a roll, it's hard to stop him.

"Bendle you missed your calling. You should have been a preacher." Mom declares.

IDK!

Dad loves to talk, especially when he's in a teaching mode. His teaching sounds more like preaching. Pulling into our driveway, he says, "When we get inside the house, I'll explain what I mean by preparing the meat, and then I'm going to bed." He goes directly to the kitchen, with Mom and me following behind.

He continues, "Remember when your grandad and I took you fishing for the first time at the Berkeley pier?"

"Mm."

"Before we left the pier, we gutted the fish, removed the scales, and washed it, right?"

"Ahhhh-hhaaaa," escapes as I nod my head in agreement.

"That's preparation! When I was a kid, meals didn't come easy. My job was to catch the chicken. I'd go to the backyard, chase a chicken until I caught it. My dad would kill it by snapping its neck and my mother took care of the rest, boiling it, removing the feathers and cutting it up to prepare for dinner. I'll never forget the first time I caught one, I couldn't eat it, but as time went on, I got over it. I had to eat what my mother put on my plate. No questions asked.

The picture of my dad chasing a chicken gets stuck in my head, it's comical, yet the thought of it being killed is grossing me out. Honestly, I've never thought about what happens to an animal before it arrives at the grocery store.

Mom interrupts. "Bendle, thought you were going to explain our tradition of eating greens on New Year's Day. You are steadily getting off topic."

"Don't worry; I'm getting to that. This is important too!" He keeps talking.

"You know meat doesn't come all cut up and nicely packaged. Someone has to slaughter the cow or pig. Catch the fish or chicken. Then prepare it for cooking. My point is made. I'm going to bed."

"What about the greens?" Mom reminds him again.

"Oh, I was getting to that."

"I'll explain it as it was explained to me by my grandfather. During the Civil War, the Union troops pillaged the land in the South. They left behind the greens and black-eyed peas because they thought it wasn't good enough for them to eat. You know the saying, 'One man's trash is another man's treasure?' It's true when it comes to the nutrients and flavor of greens.

"I wish I had more time to explain the Civil War, the Yankees, the Confederates, and the wealth acquired from our forefathers' free labor, but I'm trying to answer why we traditionally eat greens on New Year's Day. Our people yearned for better days. Every day they fought and prayed for change. The New Year marks the beginning of a new start. For our people it represents a chance for better days to come, with more resources. That means having more money. The color of the dollar is green. Eating greens stands for prosperity in the New Year. The greens are a symbol of hope and well-being. A symbol of better days to come and a spiritual connection to our ancestors."

Mom reacts, "Bendle that was the longest explanation I've heard about why we eat greens for New Year's Day."

I know my parents. This conversation is not ending here.

"Just one more example," Mom pleads.

"It will be quick, I promise."

"Don't forget about yams. They also originated in Africa. In fact, our people gave them the name. Sweet potatoes look so much like the yams grown in Africa, the slaves called American sweet potatoes 'yams,' and the name stuck. Yams grow in parts of Asia and Africa. We love yams so much that we even make pies with them!"

"Umph! Looks like your explanation is as long as mine." Dad remarks.

I can't control my yawning, "*ahhhhh-hhaaaa*."

"Just before Thanksgiving, I was watching my favorite cooking show. The chefs were demonstrating how to make pumpkin pie. Out of the clear blue, one chef says, 'A Thanksgiving without pumpkin pie is un-American.' I stopped, stared at the television in disbelief, *no, he didn't just say something so asinine and backward.* His co-host looked at him side-eyed; too bad she didn't say anything. Most Black people eat sweet potato pie, and it is as American as pumpkin pie. I'd never tasted pumpkin pie until I was an adult.

One of my colleagues was talking about how much he loved Thanksgiving, and couldn't wait to eat turkey, mash potatoes with gravy and stuffing. That conversation struck me because my family neva had mashed potatoes on Thanksgiving. We'd eat greens, mac & cheese, and yams to go with our turkey and dressing. It was obvious to me that his family's traditions differed from mine. What I'm saying is, what you eat does not define how American you are."

I really hadn't thought much about it, but she's right! My friends talk about eating all kinds of foods on Thanksgiving. Last year Markie couldn't stop bragging on his grandma's homemade tamales.

Dad declares, "You know, my favorite pie is sweet potato. I don't have to wait for a special holiday to enjoy them. I'll take a sweet potato pie over pumpkin pie any day. On that note I'm going to bed, good night."

9

ROAD TRIP
Monday Morning

WE'RE LEAVING FOR So Cal in a couple hours, and the house is surprisingly quiet. Last night Dad said he planned to go to the office to tie up a few loose ends before we leave. I packed last night, so I'm ready to leave whenever they are. Think I'll text Markie...

 What's up?

 Nothing much. My dad is doing the most, has me doin' hella chores as usual.

Reading Markie's text about his chores reminds me of how he messed up his chance to hang out with me this break. It was all set; my mom had spoken to his mom, and everything was cool. He was going to So Cal with me. Unfortunately, he got into trouble, and our plan died. Markie's mom called my mom to tell us that he couldn't go.

I heard Mom saying, "No worries, I completely understand; I would make the same decision. I agree; following directions is important. I agree; he must be accountable for his actions. It's the only way he'll learn. Right! Like I said, no worries."

Mom didn't tell me what Markie did, and neither did he, but whatever it was, his parents must have been peeved.

After Markie ruined our chance to hang out during break, I thought about asking Fola but decided not to. Even though we recently spoke, and squashed our differences, I don't want to spend the next five days with him. Besides I'm sure his parents would not allow him to come, since his grandmother is still visiting from Nigeria. Markie screwed up, so no one is coming on this trip with us.

There is a knock, knock, knocking on my door.

 Markie, I'ma hit you later.

Loudly I say, "Come in!"

Dad lets me know, "We're leaving in an hour. Are you packed and ready to go?"

"Yes."

"Good."

After dressing, I drag my suitcase downstairs, before going back up to get Mom's luggage. Next, I make sure we have Charkoal's leash, food and water bowls before grabbing something to eat.

Charkoal spends more time with Mom than she does with me, so I want another dog. My next dog will be bigger and I'm thinking a Husky will be cool. Using my laptop, I check out YouTube for Husky videos. So many videos show huskies sleeping next to babies and young children. Even though they look fierce, they must be very gentle. Convincing my mother that we need another dog will be no problem, but I don't know about my dad.

"Let's get this show on the road," Dad says upon entering the kitchen.

"Okay."

"Come help me get this luggage loaded."

After we load the luggage, Dad yells from the bottom of the stairs, "Ella, let's go!"

Finally get on the road, and it's not as boring as I thought it would be. Dad and Mom are listening to their old-school Motown jams, singing with Smokey, Aretha, and the Temptations. I kick back, texting, Snapchatting, and skimming through some hella funny TicToks, while Mom is loudly belting out, "R-E-S-P-E-C-T find out what it means to me…"

 I text my cousin Nicole, Nicky for short.
WYD cuz?

 Nothing much, waiting for you to get here. I have lots of T.

 Really, 'bout what?

 It's about this girl who's hatin' on me.

"Why?"

 "'Cause the boy she likes was tryin' to holla at me. I don't even like him. Anyways, it's drama. I'll catch you up when you get here, my dad is calling me."

 "Bet."

Nicky seems to have lots of drama at her school. She's always taking about some girl hatin' on her. Maybe she should change schools. She is my closest cousin on my dad's side, and she treats me like a brother. She trusts me and is always asking for my advice. We rarely see each other though, since we live at opposite ends of Cali. Her older brother and sister are grown and out of the house, so it's just her and Uncle Rod. She and I are closer in age, than she is to her siblings. I guess that's what makes us close. We communicate almost every day, usually via iMessage or I comment on her Instagram and TikTok videos.

As we're cruising down Interstate 5, an awful stench fills the Jeep. While mom quickly raises her window, I look over at Charkoal; her ears are flapping in the wind while her tail wags in my direction. Is the stench coming from her? From my back-seat view, I can see my dad's face in the rearview mirror. Looking seriously at me, he says, "Who farted? Whoever did it, needs to get out!"

Quick to respond, Mom retorts, "Pull over so I can let you out!"

Dad continues sternly looking at me through the mirror saying, "Wasn't me, Kyndle, don't do that again!"

I reply "It wasn't me; I didn't fart."

Chuckling, Mom joins in. "Are you sure? It smells like it's coming from the back seat. Was it Charkoal?"

Between giggles, Mom reminds me, "Don't say fart; say, 'Pass gas.' It sounds much better."

"He can say, 'Break wind, cut one, rip one, or cut the cheese.' Just say'n." Dad adds. I can't tell who's laughing more, my mom or my dad. As we pass Harris Ranch on interstate 5, there are about a thousand cows milling around.

Dad says, "There's the answer."

Mom adds, "Kyndle, excuse your dad's dry sense of humor. "

With a wide grin on his face Dad responds, "It's no fun blaming the cows."

We roll through the grapevine and are almost there. Exiting the rolling hills, a thick blanket of smog hovers over LA. I can see Magic Mountain as we descend. Finally, we arrived at our hotel. Dad goes to the lobby to check in and get our room key. This hotel is like an apartment. My parents take the upstairs loft and I get the sofa bed downstairs. I found the perfect space for Charkoal's big, round, flying-saucer-shaped doggy bed. It fits perfectly under the dining table.

Just as we finish un-packing there's knocking on the door. It's Uncle Rod and Nicky. They both enter with the widest grins on their faces. Uncle and Dad hug, Nicky greets my parents before grabbing my hand urging, "Let's go jump in the pool. I already have on my swimsuit."

Uncle Rod pretends he wants to box me saying, "Put 'em up." He softly punches me in the gut, and I pretend I'm hurt. We smile at one another when he says, "Boy you are growing like a weed." I am now a couple inches taller than him. He hugs mom asking, "How's my favorite sister-in-law?"

"Good, glad to finally be off the road. It's good to see you."

After everybody finishes greeting each other Mom says, "Bendle I need a few things from the store, I'll text you my list."

Dad says to his brother, "Take a ride with me."

Dad and Uncle Rod head out.

Nicky plays with Charkoal and talks to mom, while she waits for me to change into my swim trunks.

We stay in the water for about an hour. When we return, Dinner is ready.

It only takes me about five minutes to change and join everybody in the kitchen.

Mom set everything up buffet style, buns, hotdogs, chili, shredded cheese, mustard, catsup, pickles, and onions were all lined up. Everybody sat together after we fixed our plates.

Dad asks, "Rodney will you say grace?" Uncle Rod replies, "Sure."

Uncle Rodney is so funny, he says the shortest prayer possible, "Jesus wept."

Between bites, Dad tells Uncle Rod about my assignment, "Kyndle is working on a speech for his International Day project. He's writing about Soul food and its origin."

"Oh yeah! Have you decided what you're going to talk about?"

"Yes, I'm focusing on the foods we eat for New Year's Day that originate from Africa."

"Sounds good, what do you have so far?"

I begin reciting, "Collard Greens, Black Eyed Peas, Cornbread, Okra and Tomatoes…"

Dad interjects, "Ella did we talk about Okra yet?'

Before Mom answers, Uncle Rod tells a story, "When I was a young boy, we had to eat whatever Mama cooked, whether we liked it or not. We had to eat everything on our plates. Anyway, this one day she cooked okra and tomatoes. The moment the okra touched my tongue, I knew I was in trouble. There was no way I could eat it. It felt like slim. I said, "Ooouuu." With the look Mama gave me, I knew I wasn't getting out of it! I had to eat my food. My brothers and sisters had finished eating.

Grinning Dad says, "I remember that day."

"From the look of everyone else's plates, they liked the meal. All I could do was stare at my plate, because each time I put the fork to my mouth, I couldn't swallow it. I literally spit it back into my plate and almost got caught. Only the Lord knows what would have happened to me if my mother saw me spitting food back onto my plate. I tried everything, closing my eyes, adding more rice on the spoon and less okra and tomatoes, but nothing worked. So, when my sisters finished cleaning the kitchen, and I was left alone, I snuck out back and threw the food in the garbage can. After sneaking back in I called out, "Mama I'm finished eating." She came to the kitchen and inspected my plate. Satisfied that I had finished my dinner she instructed me to clean up after myself. After I washed my plate, fork and glass I was excused. The next morning, my mother took out some trash and found the food I'd thrown away. Boy was I in trouble. Mama made a special batch of okra and tomatoes just for me, and it was a lot. I ate it all with tears rolling down my face and some snot mixed in with my food. My mother sat and watched me eat every bite. It took me over an hour to finish it. You can believe I never tried throwing away my food again! Funny thing is, now I love okra, especially in gumbo. I even like okra and tomatoes over rice with shrimp and sausage. It must be an acquired taste. Anyway, okra originates from Africa and the word gumbo is a West African word that means okra. A lot of people don't know this. Let me think, what else can I tell you?"

Dad interrupts, "I think that's enough for tonight, let's get some rest."

I tried hard not to bust out laughing as my uncle Rod told his story. It's funny to picture him sitting at the table with my grandmother staring at him, as he cried while eating. He laughs at the end of the story, and we all join him.

As it turns out, uncle Rod and Nicky stay. Nicky sleeps on the other couch and Uncle Rod gets a sleeping bag from his car and sleeps on the floor. The following morning after breakfast we hit the road and made our first stop, Venice Beach. For the next four days we visited amusement parks and sites all over Los Angeles.

10

WELCOME BACK!
Monday, Back from Break

Dang, I'm so tired. I wish I could keep sleeping, but I can't. Tossing and turning, thinking about my paper most of the night kept me up. Feeling drowsy, I'm lying here staring at the ceiling and reading Rhianna's quote: "You may never be good enough for everybody, but you will always be the best for somebody."

Last week I knew nothing about the origin of my cultural food; now I can speak about it with confidence. I know Miss Fatona will be impressed, and I know my classmates will see that I'm no slouch!

The coffee aroma fills the air. Mom must be up, so I'd better bounce. Dragging myself out of bed, I reach for my table lamp and turn it on. Immediately Charkoal rises from her doggy bed. Her head rapidly moves and up and down and side to side like a bobblehead. The faster she moves, the more noise her collars tags make. There's an annoying cling, ting, cling, ting with her every movement. Now I'm fully awake.

Peeping through my miniblinds, I can see the clock mounted on the school steeple. It's seven o'clock. School starts in an hour and twenty. I'm yawning and stretching when someone knocks at my door. It's Mom reminding me, "It's going to be hot today, remember to take your water bottle to school and make sure you fill both doggie bowls with water. I'll meet you downstairs. Do you want a bowl of oatmeal, cereal, or a smoothie for breakfast?"

Facing the door I reply, "Smoothie please, thanks Ma.

Before dressing, I take Charkoal to the backyard so she can pee and poop. Next, I move her water and food bowls from the backyard patio into the garage where it's cooler. Charkoal follows me to the garage, I leave her there and open the doggy door so she can go outside.

Next, I rush back upstairs to get ready. Showering and thinking of what to wear, I'm torn between my purple shirt with the tan khakis or the blue shirt with blue khakis? Finally, I decide to wear my yellow polo with MOA stitched on the pocket and tan khakis with multicolored socks and my Converse sneakers.

Upon entering the kitchen, I find my parents sitting at the table.

"Good morning."

"Good morning. How'd you sleep?" asks Dad.

"I tossed and turned a lot. I'm tired."

"Hmm, after that long drive, I'm surprised you had trouble sleeping. I slept like a rock. As soon as my head hit the pillow, I was out."

"Yeah, I was thinking about what school might be like today."

Mom passes me my green smoothie stating, "I know you'll do well on your presentation because you've done all the right things to prepare. Did you get Charkoal squared away?"

"Already done."

I'm thinking, *Really, Mother, isn't it always what I do every day?*

Dad continues, "Like I always say, fail to prepare, prepare to fail. You don't have to worry about failing because you have prepared."

"Didn't I just say that, Lloyd?"

"Yeah, you did; I was just restating it a little differently."

We sit around the table eating and talking.

"It felt so good to be back in my own bed," Dad comments.

"I heard that. It's nothing like sleeping comfortably in your own home," Mom agrees.

Gulping her last bit of coffee, she places her cup in the sink.

Dad joins Mom at the sink, places his hands around her waist, and hugs and kisses her before announcing, "Have a good day. I'm taking off."

"Dad, can I catch a ride with you?"

"If you're ready now!"

"I'm ready; I just have to grab my backpack."

"And your water bottle!" Mom adds.

"Okay, hurry up! I'll be in the car."

Most mornings I catch a ride so I can get to the courts and hoop a little before the bell sounds. Mom likes getting a walk in before she starts working. Occasionally we end up walking together. Some of my friends get to school on the public AC Transit or the yellow bus. The AC bus stop is across the street from the school. The yellow bus drops kids off in front of the school, and they get clowned a lot.

Dad pulls up behind the yellow bus to drop me off. Rather than saying goodbye, he says, "Don't do anything I wouldn't do," chuckles, and tells me to have a good day. Before I close the door, he says, "Remember, you are a gentleman and a scholar. Show them what you're made of."

Smiling, I say "See ya, Dad."

I close the car door and follow the crowd of students walking onto the campus. Inside building A, I weave through the crowd, twisting, zigzagging, and turning to navigate my way through the horde of students. Reaching my destination, I turn the black dial from right to left, then right again. It lands on number 12, and I lift up the silver handle. It doesn't open. Sighing, I start over. Turning the knob right to 10, left past 10 to 24, then right to 12. I hear a click, and this time when I lift the silver handle, the door opens. After grabbing my history book, I slam the gray metal door shut and run through the less-crowded hallway. Two girls slowly stride with large backpacks protruding from their backs; I go around them. Before I reach my class, I see a group of eighth-grade boys huddled in the middle of the hallway, they must be ignoring the bell. Whew, made it to class. I'm not late! Miss Fatona is standing at the door, propping it open with her tall, skinny body. Breathing heavily, I greet her. "Hi, Miss Fatona."

Smiling, she says, "Welcome back, Kyndle."

Miss Fatona moves away from the door as I enter, and it closes behind her. Today she's wearing what my mom calls her limo driver outfit. Black jeans, a pair of no-name black sneakers, and a white shirt. Practically every day she wears a white shirt with a pearl necklace and either blue, black, or white jeans. I must have grown some over break, because it doesn't feel like Miss Fatona is towering over me.

Wonder if I have caught up to Fola? He's the tallest boy in sixth grade at five feet seven inches, beating me by an inch. Because of my height, most people think that I'm already in high school. For this reason, among others, I can't wait to get there.

Everything in class looks just as we left it. In the rear corner is the big metal box on wheels that stores our Chromebooks. My Stephen Curry bobblehead is exactly where I left it: on top of my desk. While Miss Fatona opens the windows, the class is buzzing with conversations about what they did last week during spring break.

Written on the whiteboard in big, bold letters are the words "Welcome back!" In place of an exclamation point is an upside-down daisy with a long green stem and bright-pink flower at the bottom. Miss Fatona always does a little extra to brighten our day. Before speaking, she perches her cat-eye-shaped glasses on the end of her snubby honey-colored nose.

"Everybody take your seat; it's time to get to work. I trust you all enjoyed your time off. Before we dive in, who wants to share what you did over break?"

The classroom is silent; nobody responds.

Miss Fatona reminds us, "Class participation counts toward your grade."

Like everyone else's hand, mine shoots up!

"I thought that would get your attention. Who wants to go first?"

The only hand still raised was Tinah's.

Before speaking she starts coughing. "Ahem, ahem. I hung out, ahem, ahem, with my cousins. We were at the R Ranch with my grandparents. We swam a lot, ahem, and went horseback riding practically every day."

"Sounds like you caught a cold. Did you sleep outside in a tent?" asks Miss Fatona.

"No, we were in a cabin and slept in sleeping bags."

"Sounds like you had a really good time. Thanks for sharing, Tinah. Hope you feel better soon, and take care of that cough."

Practically everybody finished sharing about camping, swimming, visiting amusement parks, and hanging out with relatives before it was my turn to speak.

"My family took a road trip to Southern California. We went to Disneyland, Knott's Berry Farm, Venice Beach, Santa Monica Beach and Hollywood Boulevard with my uncle and cousin. It was all good."

"I'm glad you all enjoyed your time off. Let's move this discussion forward and talk about our program."

Fola's long, skinny, ebony-colored arm starts flinging to get Miss Fatona's attention. He blurts out, "You forgot me!"

"I'm sorry. I didn't mean to overlook you, Fola. Go ahead. Share with us."

IDK!

"My grandmother is still visiting from Nigeria, so we took her to the city and did some sightseeing and shopping. We rode the cable cars and every night a bunch of friends and relatives stopped by to play mancala—it's an African game—and listened to my uncle tell African fables. He's a good storyteller."

"Thanks for sharing that. It's so nice that you are spending time with your grandmother. Quality time with family and friends makes for good memories. Did I miss anyone else?"

Tony raises his hand. "Tony, didn't you share already?"

"Yes. I have a question. What did you do over the break?"

Miss Fatona seems caught off guard and nervously laughs before answering, "Relaxed mostly. I slept in every day. Took a stroll to the neighborhood coffee shop, walked my dogs, Bambi, Teeny, and Kitty. I met up with friends, and before I knew it, it was over. I'm happy to be back with all of you. We have much work ahead of us, so let's get to it!

Before break, we discussed your International Day assignment. Each of you will bring a dish to share, give a speech that's no less than 3 minutes and no longer than 10; also submit no less than two typed written pages day after tomorrow. Any questions?"

Kiko raises her hand. "If we don't have a printer at home, can we print our paper here?"

"Yes. I'll print your papers for you if you don't have a printer. Use the rest of today to put the finishing touches on your speeches."

I take Chromebook number 22 from the docking charging cart to look up more facts and fine tune my draft. Google Drive makes it easy for me to work on my paper at home and in class.

I find an article about Nelson Mandela, apartheid, and civil rights in America. The article compared the American civil rights movement to South Africa's apartheid. I'm shocked by the similarities. Laws were created to legally mistreat Black people here and there. I don't find much that I would include in my paper, but it is worth reading. Everyone is silently reading and writing. Just before the bell sounds, Miss Fatona tells us, "Gather your belongings; class will be dismissed shortly. Kyndle, see me after class."

I'm thinking, *Now what?*

Within seconds, Miss Fatona and I are the only two left in the classroom. She asks me, "How are you feeling about your speech?"

"Good."

"That's great to hear."

"I've got my village."

"Oh?"

"My parents, grandparents and uncle told me so many stories and shared some good information about our food. I did my own research too. I'm prepared."

With her palm up, Miss Fatona sticks her hand out and waits for me to give her five. I don't leave her hanging when I slide the palm of my hand against hers. She responds, "Now that's what I'm talkin' 'bout."

Relieved, I relax when Miss Fatona code switches. Most often she speaks formally, but occasionally she switches up and speaks to me like I'm family. This is one of those times. She's always stressing the importance of knowing the difference between speaking Standard English, colloquial, and slang. According to Miss Fatona, it's most important to know when to switch. It's

IDK!

clear to me now how she is part of my village. Praising me, she reminds me of my mother. Miss Fatona is cool. Smiling warmly, she compliments me: "I'm happy to see those brown eyes sparkle again."

Appreciating her comment, I reply, "Thanks."

Whew! I'm glad this meeting was short and sweet, because Krishna, Markie and Fola are waiting for me on the blacktop. Since Fola and I spoke over break, we're cool again.

My boys and I decide to play a game of horse. My game is off for some reason; I attempt to copy Krishna's sky hook and miss. Dang, I already have an *H*. I lose because I spell H-O-R-S-E first by missing too many copycat shots. Now I'm out of the game. Instead of standing around watching my boys, I walk over to where some girls are in a circle, listening to music and dancing. Maria stops. "Hi, Kyndle."

She comes over to where I am, and pauses before asking, "Are you still mad at me?" "I didn't mean to hurt your feelings. I didn't really think Soul food was from Seoul, Korea. I was just trying to be funny. You seemed really nervous, so I tried to lighten things up."

"Oh, I didn't know what was up. Your question didn't make me feel any better." With a friendly grin, I say, "Next time don't do me any favors."

"So do you accept my apology?" Maria asks.

"It's all good."

I'm glad Maria is taking the time to explain why she did what she did. Asking me if Soul food was from Seoul, Korea, felt out of pocket since she knows I'm American. Everyone's bringing their cultural food, and my tightly coiled coarse hair, caramel skin tone, and swagger make it pretty obvious I'm Black. Maria and I are friends and competitors; we are both in the top five percent of sixth graders at MOA.

As I'm walking away, heading back toward the courts, Maria calls out, "Do you want to be my partner for our ancient world history assignment?"

I call back, "Um, I guess."

The game of H-O-R-S-E is just ending. Krishna won.

"We've got time for another game," Markie says.

Ready to redeem myself I say, "I'm in."

Krishna gets to take the first shot, because he won the last game. He misses. I get the rebound. With a slight twist and skyhook my first shot goes in. Swoosh! I'm off to a good start. I toss the ball to Markie. He has to attempt my exact shot. Looks like Markie's skyhook needs some work. He misses, and it's Fola's turn. The bell sounds. Everyone clears the yard, heading to their last-period class.

11

THE FIRST HUMANS!
Monday, Last Period

MARKIE AND I catch up to some friends who are walking toward science class.

Kiko, Jose, Krishna, Markie, Tinah, and I have science together. Just as I reach the line, Mr. Blackwell opens the door. His old-school 1970s Afro is the bomb. It's so neat—combed out and trimmed perfectly like Eddie Murphy's 'fro in *Dr. Doolittle*. Mr. Blackwell stands at the entry door with his iPad in hand, taking attendance as we file in. I walk in behind Kiko, and we both greet Mr. Blackwell.

I pull out a chair from beneath the rectangular-shaped table and place my jacket on it to stake my claim. We don't have assigned seats in the lab; it's all first come, first served. The connected tables are in a *U* shape, and surrounding walls are covered with upper and lower cabinets that are filled with supplies. Mr. Blackwell speaks, "This week we will continue learning how DNA replicates itself through the process of creating base pairs. All living creatures as we know them have genetic information that is passed down through DNA.

Supplies for today's experiment are sitting on the tables: beakers, cups, pitchers of water, bottles of alcohol, cotton cloth, cartons of fresh strawberries, and sandwich bags." Providing instruction, Mr. Blackwell proceeds, "We're going to extract DNA from strawberries. Put on your lab coats and safety goggles before we get started. Take one strawberry, and pass the carton down. Next place the strawberry inside the plastic sandwich bag. Use the alcohol wipe to clean your hands after placing the strawberry in the bag. We're going to make the extraction solution using a beaker, water, shampoo, and salt."

Tinah jokes, "Markie betta save some of that shampoo for his head."

Everyone hearing Tinah, busted out laughing. Knowing how foul it is to be the butt of someone's joke, I don't join in the laughter, even though it was hella funny. Markie tried to play it off by laughing too, but I know he didn't like it.

Unaware of what was said during the outburst, Mr. Blackwell quickly brings order to the class stating sternly, "Cool it!"

He continues giving instructions, then announces that he has a meeting, and a substitute teacher will be arriving shortly. "Please be on your best behavior for the sub. I'll ask her to list the names of any student who is disruptive, so don't think you can get away with anything while I'm gone."

"Where you going, Mr. Blackwell?" Jose asked.

"I have a union meeting."

IDK!

"Any more questions before the sub arrives? Speak now or forever hold your peace." He chuckles. "Tomorrow we will use our pipette or tweezers to remove the DNA from the test tube. Be sure to label your tube, hang up your lab coats, clean your area, and put away the supplies. Microscopes will be used to look more closely at the DNA."

A light-skinned, dark-haired lady walks through the door, and Mr. Blackwell greets her with a smile. He quickly speaks to her, then introduces her to us. "Class, this is Mrs. Beaker. She'll be with you for the next forty minutes. Please pay attention and be respectful."

She looks like a combination of Asian and Black or Latina. As soon as he leaves, she reintroduces herself. "You can call me Mrs. Beaker or Mrs. B. When addressing me, please remember to say 'Mrs.' For the remainder of class today, we will discuss the cradle of humankind. Let's have a little fun."

I think I like her already.

Mrs. B. takes a bunch of name tags and begins passing them to students sitting at the front of each row. She directs us. "Take a tag, then pass the rest to the person sitting behind you."

A few kids start talking. Mrs. B. warns, "It's important that you listen carefully and follow my instructions in order for this game to work."

She gets our attention. "Do not speak until instructed to do so. Now take the tag and write the name of your favorite cartoon character or famous person, and place it on the back of the person in front of you. If you're sitting in the front row, go to the person sitting at the back of your row, and place the tag on his or her back.

You'll have five minutes to ask each other a maximum of three questions. For example: Am I a woman? Am I an animal? Am I an athlete? Your answers must be yes or no! No open-ended questions allowed.

Krishna raises his hand. Mrs. B points to Krishna, "Go ahead."

Krishna asks. "What's an open-ended question?"

"For example, how is your day going is an open-ended question. It allows you to give a lengthy answer versus a closed ended question, is you day going good or bad? The person answering the question is given two choices, one or the other. Does this make sense?"

"Yes, thank you," Krishna smiles.

Mrs. B continues, "The first person to figure out the name on his or her back is the winner and will have the privilege of being my co-teacher for the balance of class today. Are there any questions?"

No hands rise.

Mrs. B. looks at the clock on the wall. When the second hand reaches the number six, she says, "Go!"

We all quickly run around the room, asking each person three questions.

"Am I a person?"

"Am I a cartoon character?"

"Am I popular?"

"Am I a thing?"

"Am I on television?"

"Do I wear special clothing?"

"Am I a star?"

"Do adults like me?"

Jose figures out the name on his back is Spider-Man. He wins! Cool game! When Jose goes to the front of the class to join Mrs. B., she points to her seat and motions for Jose to take it.

"Please open your human biology textbook to chapter seven, '*Homo Sapiens* and Early Human Migration.'"

Mrs. B. begins, "Between two and three hundred thousand years ago, the first humans evolved from Africa. They began moving outside of the African continent about seventy to one hundred thousand years ago and migrated to Asia and Europe..."

About ten minutes before class ends, Mrs. B. finishes lecturing and tells Jose, "Your turn. It's time for you to lead the class discussion."

Jose begins by saying, "From here I can see who has African lips, noses, skin color, and hair." Then he starts calling out, "Krishna, you and Fola are both chocolate, and he is from Africa. Kiko, you have an African nose and lips. Markie, you have African lips..." Before Krishna, Kiko, or Markie react, the entire class bursts into uncontrollable laughter. Kiko's beige complexion and Markie's cream coffee skin tone, both turn hot red. Krishna simply looks mad. "I am Indian, not African," he says.

Then Markie yells, "Jose you have African hair. Your fro is as big as Mr. Blackwell's."

Mrs. B. speaks, and the class calms down. "What did we learn from the lesson? Humans migrated from Africa thousands of years ago. That being said, we are all African, and technically race is a social construct. Which means there's only one race. Humans! It was not until the eighteenth century, during the conquering of Native Americans and the African slave trade, that Europeans began using the term 'race' to categorize people by skin color and other features. The topic of social constructs will be taught when you are in seventh grade. For today's discussion, we're stickin' to the evolution of mankind.

There is no such thing as African lips or noses. Most people think White people have long, pointy noses, and people of African descent have short, wide noses. Truth is, most nose shapes can be found among various ethnic groups. The human nose uses both length and nostril shape to efficiently regulate body temperature in different climates. It's assumed the first Africans mostly had short noses with round nostrils since it was very hot in Africa. When Africans ventured off into colder climates, the nostrils became narrower. Since Europe is colder than Africa, Europeans tend to have a higher prevalence of pointed noses. Many Africans living in colder climates have longer, pointed noses as well. One type is not better than the other. Do we need to discuss this subject more?"

No one says a thing until Krishna asks, "What about lips? Why are some thick and some are thin?"

Mrs. B. answers, "It's all in DNA. You'll learn more about it when Mr. Blackwell returns." She continues, "Jose, thank you for being my co-teacher today; you may return to your seat now."

Mrs. B. has turned out to be a pretty cool sub.

As Kiko, Jose, Markie, Tinah, and I exit the classroom, Jose tells Kiko, "I wasn't trying to make a joke. Y'all took it wrong. I'm proud of my African roots, and everyone should be, just like Mrs. Beaker said. Besides my papá told me, that the second president of Mexico, Vicente Guerrero was mixed race like President

Obama. He was a African Mexican and a distant relative. That makes me part Black."

Tinah sneezes before asking, "How is that like our first Black President? Obama isn't Mexican."

"We know, but he was mixed race like Vincente Guerrero, his mother was European, and his father was from Africa."

Tinah quickly sneezes into her arm, "Achoo," then says, "Look who's tryin' to sound like the teacher."

Jose responds, "I got it like that. Just giving y'all some more knowledge!"

As Jose talks, I'm thinking about the beginning of humankind and how it all started in Africa. Maybe I should add something about the African migration throughout the world to my Soul food speech, on second thought, it might be too long.

Tinah responds to Jose, "I ain't mad at you."

Changing the subject, Markie asks, "Tinah, why you gotta come for me?"

"Huh? What are you talkin' 'bout?"

"Why did you say I need to save some shampoo for my head?"

Immediately Tinah's face develops a scowl and she's looking mean, "Oh, you still thinking about that. Why you gotta be so effin' sensitive, Markie? I was just kidding. Lighten up!"

"It's not cool."

Tinah can tell that Markie is serious. Her face softens when she apologizes, "My bad. I didn't mean anything by it. I was just having a little fun."

Markie begs, "Well, I'd 'preciate it if you didn't front me. What you said was wack!"

Jose, still in teacher mode, says, "Y'all need to quit beefin'."

Guess Tinah heard because she turned to Markie with seriousness and stated, "My bad. I got you, Markie. I'm really sorry."

Glad that's squashed.

Some of my friends head to the yellow bus, others to the AC Transit, and a few to their parents' cars. I walk around the corner, and I'm home.

12

LESS THAN 24 HOURS
Tuesday Morning

THE BANGING ON my door startles me. "Kyndle, you overslept. Get up! This is not the day to be late." As if an electric current runs through my body, I sit straight up!

Dang! I can't believe I overslept. Last night I stayed up late putting the finishing touches on my paper to make it perfect. Now I've got to rush to shower and get dressed. Getting dressed quickly, I check my backpack to make sure I have my paper.

Stepping into the kitchen, where Mom is waiting for me, I grab my smoothie from the counter, and we head out the door. Arriving at school a few minutes before the bell sounds, I quickly hug Mom before getting out of the car.

"Enjoy your day. See you when I get home. Oh, and don't forget to put the trash bins up."

"Okay, you have a good day too Ma." I quickly walk toward my classroom. On minimum days I only have two classes: science and history.

Something seems off this morning. It's 8:30 A.M. and Mr. Blackwell is sitting at his desk reading the morning paper. By this time, he's usually talking to us about something he read in a scientific journal. It's unusual for him to sit quietly.

Finally Mr. Blackwell speaks after everyone has put away their coats and backpacks. "Did you all enjoy the discussion about *Homo sapiens* and early human migration with Mrs. Beaker? Would anyone like to share thoughts about the lesson?"

Jose raises his hand. "I was her assistant, so I'll share. Thousands of years ago, Africans started migrating to other parts of the world. They went to the Middle East and Asia. What I'm trying to figure out is, if Africans are Black, and they migrated to other places around the world, why do we have so many different colors of people? Does this mean all Africans didn't have dark skin?"

"Very good question, Jose. People typically think of Africans as having darker skin, but Africans come in all shades, from very light beige to black. Some scientists believe as Africans migrated farther from the equator, they evolved lighter skin as an adaptation to limited sunlight. Also, melanin, the skin's darker pigment, is a natural sunscreen that protects the skin from harmful ultraviolet (UV) rays. We'll have more discussions on genetics and skin color diversity in the future. Are there any other comments or questions before you take your DNA quiz? Yes, Kiko?"

"Mrs. B said," Kiko looks at her notes, "Race is a social construct. What exactly does that mean, Mr. Blackwell?"

"The short answer is that humans divided people into different races in the mid-17th century, to justify slavery of Africans in colonial America. Unfortunately, it's not a subject that I teach, and you'll have the opportunity to learn more in seventh and eighth grade. Any more comments or questions?"

Kiko states, "I liked the way Mrs. B. played a game with us before we started serious work. Do you think we can start playing games too?"

"I'm certainly open to it. Why don't you develop a plan and present it to me when we meet next, and I'll consider it? Now for today's quiz. The extra credit question is worth five points. Good luck! If you finish early, please work quietly at your desk. Those of you who are presenting tomorrow for International Day can work on your speeches."

After seeing the first question:

Nitrogen bases pair with _____ bases.

a. available
b. complimentary
c. identical
d. both b and c

I circle *b*.

The rest of the quiz is a breeze. Confident that I have answered the questions correctly, I place my pencil on my desk and relax while a few others are still finishing their quizzes. Within a few minutes, Mr. Blackwell says, "Time's up. Pass your quizzes forward." After he collects them, he says, "You all are dismissed."

On minimum days the hallways are more crowded. The lunchroom is louder, with trays clashing and lips smacking. Everyone seems to be rushing to get food and scarf it down since we only get twenty-five minutes for lunch instead of our normal fifty minutes. After taking the last bite of my apple, I head to room 23 for history.

TUESDAY AFTERNOON

It's 12:10 p.m., and Miss Fatona is reading something on her iPad while Krishna and Markie talk about Curry's NBA finals performance, Kiko and Tinah are chatting about what they plan to wear tomorrow, and Jose and I are laughing loudly at Maria's joke. Miss Fatona finally says to us, "Take your seats, and pass your papers to the front."

After she collects papers from everyone, she reminds us, "Class will be dismissed at 1:45 p.m. While I read your speeches, you may find a book to read or play online games."

Jose says to Pierre, "Let's play Kahoot!"

Miss Fatona continues speaking, "You can also check out upcoming assignments in Google Classroom, practice exercises using IXL or Khan Academy, or get a head start on your ancient world history project; it's your choice."

I call out to Tinah, "Hey, want to play Scrabble?"

Before answering, she barely gets the words out, "Ahem, ahem, ahem, you must be in the mood to get your butt kicked."

Miss Fatona notices Tinah coughing and says to her, "You need to get that checked out."

"You're right Miss Fatona, ahem, ahem I will."

The challenge is on. I grab the board game from the cabinet. We both reach inside the bag and pull out a tile. I get a Q; it's worth ten points. Tinah pulls an *S*; it's only worth one point, so I go first.

Around 1:30 pm Miss Fatona announces, "These speeches are excellent. I've learned so much from reading them, and I'm proud of each of you. Because of your hard work and dedication, I know this year's International Day will be ranked among the best. I've made my comments; you'll see them written in red ink. When I call your name, please come forward and collect your paper."

"Kiko, Maria, Krishna, Markie, Fola, Jose, Kyndle, Tony, Tinah……..." The speeches are in the author's hands. There are lots of smiles on faces. When I see the A+ written at the top of my paper in bright-red ink, I can't help but grin from ear to ear.

The classroom fills with loud chatter as everyone proudly shares their grade.

International Day is now less than twenty-four hours away. Instead of shooting hoops after school, I choose to go home.

When I step inside, I'm surprised to see my dad sitting in the office. He seems surprised to see me too; I guess he forgot that today is a minimum day. Just as I am about to say hi, he quickly puts his index finger over his lips, shhhh! Recently Dad got new earbuds, and it's hard to tell when he's on the phone. He continues talking, telling the person on the other end, "It's practically done. I have one final meeting with the CFO and CEO to seal the deal. At this point it's a formality."

While Dad talks business, I check out my paper, making a mental note of Miss Fatona's comment: "Great work! Speeches should range from three to no more than ten minutes."

Dad finishes his conversation and says, "How was school today?"

I hold up my paper so he can see the A+ for himself and read the comment.

Dad extends his fist and gives me pound out of respect for my work. "I'm proud of you. I told you, you got this! Now all you have to do is make sure it's not too long. You deserve to relax. Don't worry about the trash bins or taking care of Charkoal; I got you."

Man, I wasn't expecting that. "Thanks, Dad."

"Hey, you earned it. I'll get your chores squared away; then I'm taking a Zoom meeting, so my office door will be closed."

I go to my room, lie across my bed, and fall asleep. After about an hour of sleeping, I take a nice hot shower.

Refreshed, I get comfortable and put on a pair of sweats, then grab one of Mom's power bars and a bottle of Gatorade to drink.

Time for revisions. First, I listen to a couple of my favorite songs: "Started From the Bottom," by Drake; an old favorite by Migos, "Walk It Talk It"; and "Hurricane," by Kanye, featuring Lil Baby and The Weeknd. I'm pumped. I set my cell phone timer to ten minutes. Next I begin reading my speech aloud, to make sure I'm within the allotted time. When my ten minutes are up, I have a little over a paragraph left to read. I count the number of words to determine how many I need to get rid of. I read it again, this time with my finger on the delete button. I've deleted about a hundred words. It shouldn't be too long now.

For some reason, my grandmother's favorite spiritual comes to mind, "I Don't Believe He Brought Me This Far to Leave Me." When she's cooking and cleaning, she's usually singing or humming the words to this song. Now I find myself doing the same thing as I make changes to my speech.

My forefathers sang to ease their pain, as they worked in the fields, picking crops ranging from tobacco to cotton and sugarcane to coffee beans. They came in bondage to the New World. Over time they lost their languages, but many of their customs remained. They came to North, Central, and South America as skilled manufacturers, artisans, and architects and brought with them their cultures, food, languages, and faith systems.

Many African artists used gold, bronze, brass, copper, and ivory to make beautiful crafts. Northwest Africans, called Moors by the Spanish, were scholars, engineers, and great builders. African kings and chiefs sold their prisoners into slavery, not knowing how people would be tortured. Slavery in Africa was not brutal nor torturous as it was in America.

Africans were carried by cargo ships, shackled in chains at the legs, necks, and wrists with heavy irons. They were stowed in the lower ship decks, packed like sardines. Fifteen to twenty million people were sold into slavery and transported to the West Indies.

Preparing for this day, I learned the African proverb "It takes a village." My village taught me that Soul food is about love. My ancestors worked so hard, from "Can't see in the morning" to "Can't see at night." They toiled in fields from dark to dark. If there was enough moonlight, they were forced to continue working.

Their meals were made from scraps of leftovers controlled by slaveholders. Many suffered from malnutrition. Mealtime was a special time because food not only fed the belly, it also fed the Soul.

My mother reminds me that our forefathers were given lemons and made lemonade. They took the meager scraps given to them and made delicacies.

Savory foods like chitlins are traditionally eaten on New Year's Day for good luck. I now understand how eating the most undesirable parts of the pig brought good luck. People were able to survive by eating these scraps high in nutrients. Therefore, high protein chitlins were a blessing. Luck comes from God's grace.

Today we are politicians, activists, lawyers, judges, doctors, scientists, engineers, entertainers, scholars, and business professionals. We have come very far despite obstacles put in our way, yet we have a long way to go! My grandmother would say, "Ump, ump, ump, We've Come This Far By Faith, Leaning On The Lord."

Tuesday Evening

Just after I make my final edit, the front door opens. "Kyndle." It's Mom calling me.

"Yeah Ma?"

The kitchen door swings open, and my mother manages to make it to the island without dropping any of the bags in her hands or the one tucked under her arm. Placing them down, she sighs! "Phew, go get the rest of the groceries."

The Jeep is filled with bags of fresh collard greens, yams, fruits, vegetables, spices, and cans of salmon. I grab three bags, leaving two more in the car. Returning to the kitchen, I see my mother has her apron on, and she's ready to clean the greens. Water is filling the kitchen sink as she places bunches into the water. Making my final trip to the car, I grab the last two bags. When I return, Mom says, "Text your dad and ask him to pick up some Chinese food for dinner."

IDK!

"Okay." While I look for my phone, Mom asks, "So how are you feeling about your speech?"

I simply held up my graded paper and let it speak for itself.

"Wow! A-plus...that's fantastic. I knew you could do it! I am so proud of you! So what are you doing now?"

"Removing words to make sure I don't go over ten minutes when speaking."

"Well, all right then."

"I've been practicing aloud, and I think I've finally got it down."

"That's great. Want to practice with me?"

"Um, no thanks. I want you to be surprised."

Sighing she sings, "Okay. I understand."

"It didn't really feel like hard work. The research I did helped me change my attitude about slavery. Instead of feeling ashamed, I feel proud of what my people have accomplished and contributed to our country. People who force others into bondage are the ones who need to change. My speech is going to be fire. I'll give the audience something to think about. As Dad would say, truth be told."

My mother's eyes are starting to glisten. I think, *Oh no, don't start crying*. She comes toward me looking as though she's holding back tears. Thankfully, I don't see any.

"Let me give you a hug."

"You sure are maturing into a fine young man and an independent thinker. You will be told a lot of things about your history, your race, and who you are. It's important to learn as much as you can about your ancestry. For that matter, any subject, so you can make informed decisions for yourself. Nobody has all of the right answers. Knowledge will strengthen you!"

I notice her eyes are locked in on something behind me.

She says, "You see that bag on the chair? Go open it; there's something in it for you."

It's the bag she had tucked under her arm. Opening the bag, I find two vibrant matching multicolored garments, one my size, the other bigger. I'm guessing it's for my dad. Both look like works of art. Bright red, royal blue, green, and yellow create a geometric pattern. The V–neck collars are covered with squiggly gold thread in circles, curves, and lines. "Wow! Thanks, Ma." This time I give her a hug.

"I thought it would be nice for you and your father to wear matching outfits."

"This is really cool."

"Yeah, I think it's time to get your dad out of his business suit." We both laugh.

"He needs a new dashiki. The one he has is old, and it needs to be retired. He still wears it to every event where the dress code is African attire. It's time for it to be donated, so we can bless someone else."

Researching for this project has made me eager to know more about all things African, so I ask, "Where does the word 'dashiki' come from?

"It's a Yoruba word meaning 'shirt.'" Pointing to the outfits, she adds, "Those are from Nigeria. It's in West Africa."

"I know. West Africans were part of the slave trade."

"Of course, you know that, Mr. Smarty Pants." She clowns around with me a little.

My cell vibrates. It's my dad replying to my earlier text. "On my way home with Chinese food."

"Do you need me to help with anything before I go upstairs?"

"No, thanks. You deserve to relax."

Lying on my back with my red Beats by Dre in my ears, I listen to Dom Kennedy. "You get what you put in…" Dom speaks my language.

With closed eyes, I listen to more upbeat music as I envision myself standing on stage in my African outfit. The audience is going crazy with applause as I take a bow.

My door opens before I notice. My eyes adjust, and I look up to find my dad standing in my doorway. "Kyndle, how many times do I have to tell you not to have that music too loud? You're going to burst your eardrums with all that loud music. Dinner is ready."

"Okay, thanks."

Seven white takeout boxes with red Chinese writing are sitting on the table. Something for everybody. Dad likes the kung pao shrimp without nuts. I like orange chicken. Mom's favorites are dry string beans and eggplant. We always get rice, chow mein, egg rolls, and pot stickers. Paper plates are already on the table. I volunteer, "I'll say grace."

Mom looks pleased, and Dad says with a big grin, "Go for it; the honor is yours."

I feel a stronger connection to my heritage. One that I didn't have before this assignment. I've always been thankful for my family, but this is different. Maybe it's the knowledge that my ancestors didn't have the privilege of staying together. That their families were broken apart. I can't imagine being taken away from my family and never seeing them again. I see things differently. I'm viewing my own family in a whole new light. Closing my eyes with my head bowed, I clasp my hands together, giving honor to God. "Dear God, thank you for this day. Thank you for my parents, grandparents, and forefathers who came to this country with nothing, making a way out of no way, as my granny would say. Thank you for giving my ancestors strength and fortitude, making them survivors. Thank you for giving them the power of prayer, hope, and belief that better days would come. If it were not for the strength you gave to them, we would not be here today. Thank you for the food we are about to receive for our bodies' nourishment. Thank you for the food we enjoy today, created by our ancestors in their new homeland, as native Black Americans. Amen!"

Opening my eyes, I find my parents staring at me as though starstruck. "Aaamen. That was excellent."

"Thanks, Ma."

"Kyndle, you hit that one out of the ballpark. Seriously, that was a beautiful prayer."

"Thanks." We each take a box, spoon food onto our plates, and pass the boxes around as we inhale a medley of aromas. Competing scents fill the kitchen. From the Chinese food we are scarfing down to the simmering collard greens, sweet yams baking, and the holy trinity of base ingredients—onions, bell peppers, and celery—sautéing on the stove.

Shortly after we finish eating, the doorbell rings. Looking through the peephole, I see it's my granny and grandad. When I open the door, we all greet one another at the same time.

Grandad's hands are full. I take a couple bags from him to help. He greets me, "How you doin'?"

"Good," I reply as we make our way to the kitchen.

As Mom clears the kitchen table, Granny greets her. "How's it going, Ella?"

"Good, Mother Shirley. Have you eaten yet? We have plenty of Chinese food left."

"No, thank you, Ella; we ate already. How have you been?"

"Busy as usual, Mother Shirley."

Mom greets Grandad. "How you doin', Pops?"

Grandad answers, "Doin' fine, Ella," as he places a large bag filled with stacks of pie shells on the kitchen counter. While the women work diligently in the kitchen, the men retreat to the family room to watch the all-star game.

Granny's looking around the kitchen. She opens the oven door and notices the pans of golden cornbread. "Ella, I think it's time to take this cornbread out."

"Can you take it out for me?"

"Sure."

"Thank you."

Granny puts on ovens mitts, before taking the golden hot cornbread from the oven. Next, she puts the two large pans on the counter to cool. After taking the mitts off, she carefully reaches into the large zipped insulated container and takes pie shells out one at a time.

"Your crust looks perfect!" Mom compliments Granny. "One of these days, I hope to get my pie crust edges to look like yours. They're always perfectly molded, like fine ceramic art."

Granny smiles. She prides herself on making the prettiest, flakiest, best-tasting pie crust in the family. Still poking around, she checks out the greens simmering on the stove. Next, she opens the bottom oven and uses a fork to pierce the yams, checking to see it they are ready to come out. Suddenly she says, "Where's the meat?"

"Don't worry, Bendle's mixture for the croquettes is in the refrigerator."

Dad yells from the adjacent family room, "My stuff is tight. Everything is mixed, and in the fridge. I'm cooking them in the morning."

"Tight?"

"Mother, you have to stay current. This is young folks' lingo."

"Then please explain to me why you're using it? You are not young, Lloyd." Everybody cracks up. Granny's got jokes too.

Dad responds, "I'm just keeping my skills sharp."

Granny says, "Well, I'm happy to see you all have got it together. Oops! I mean tight. Guess I need to work on my lingo too."

13

INTERNATIONAL DAY
Wednesday

LYING IN BED with closed eyes, I wake up before my alarm chimes. Maybe it is the faint aroma of spicy sizzling salmon croquettes that awakens me or maybe the excitement of the day. My room is completely dark except for the bright light emitting from my cell phone. It's 6:20 a.m., twenty-five minutes before my alarm clock is set to go off. With time to spare, I send a group text to wish my friends good luck today. Rapidly, responses pour in; guess I'm not the only one up early. Everybody is juiced.

At the foot of my bed, in place of my uniform, is my multicolored Nigerian dashiki with matching pants. It feels weird putting it on; I'm so used to wearing my school uniform. Looking at myself in the mirror, I hope I don't look as silly as I feel.

When I enter the kitchen, Dad and I look at each other and can't help laughing out loud. It feels strange being dressed alike, it's as though I'm seeing an older version of myself.

"Do you need help?"

Dad is placing the last batch of croquettes into the pan before covering with foil.

"No, I got it thanks."

"Before you put them all in, I want a couple."

Dad removes all but four from the skillet and places the rest in the pan. I take two and put two on a small plate for Mom.

Biting into the perfectly round shaped, flavorful crispy moist patty, I sighed, "Ump, ump ump! This is so good. These are fire."

"I aim to please. Besides some folks have never tasted croquettes and I want to keep them coming back for more," he says confidently.

Changing the subject I say, "You know Dad, I researched that African people dress alike to signify their unity. They also dress alike for special occasions, like weddings, funerals, graduations and to show their spirituality or social status. So, we're right on time with the clothes Mom got for us."

"You know, people in the south typically do the same thing. Families will wear matching colors or outfits for funerals, reunions and other special occasions. One year I bought your mother and I matching pants and shirts, we were celebrating her birthday." Dad ponders, "Wonder if these customs were passed down from our ancestry?"

Thinking aloud I say, "Wonder what's taking Ma so long. She's usually in the kitchen before us?"

Just then, she enters looking regal. Dad and I are in awe!

"Wow, you look gorgeous." Dad compliments.

Agreeing, "Yeah I like you fit."

With a huge smile on her face she replies, "Thank you."

Her head is adorned with a sparkly gold headdress with splashes of red, green, and black, that match the red and green in our dashikis.

Her blouse and skirt have the same geometric pattern as ours. We keep admiring her. Dad pays another compliment, "You look really elegant, Ella."

Still smiling radiantly, she repeats, "Thank you."

"I'm wearing a Nigerian head tie called a *gele*."

Grinning even more, she says, "I'd give you both a big kiss, but I don't want to mess up my lipstick."

Glancing at the oven clock, Mom asks, "Is the food in the car?"

"Yes, dear." Dad responds.

Mom takes a cup of yogurt from the fridge to eat in the car. With a few minutes to spare, we take a few selfies before walking out the door.

The parking lot at Michelle Obama Academy is filling up quickly. Dad gets lucky; a red Corvette pulls out of the space just ahead, and he grabs it. The car engine turns off, and I begin feeling nauseous. To take my mind off my queasiness, I think about how good the food will taste, but it barely helps my jitters. I see Kiko's parents getting out of their silver minivan. Kiko is wearing a beautiful pink kimono with a pattern of flying birds in red and gold. We wave to each other warmly, as I help my dad load two pans of his delicious salmon croquettes into my old red Radio Flyer wagon. There's no room left in the wagon after we put the 20-gallon stainless steel pot of greens inside, so looks like we have to make two trips.

Dad pulls the heavy wagon to the Mark Zuckerberg multipurpose room, which is located next to the Dr. Mark E. Dean library. Kiko's family walks with mine, and her dad is wheeling a large blue igloo cooler.

"Cool outfit, Kiko. What's in the cooler?"

"Thanks, Kyndle! I like yours too. Don't you remember? I'm bringing sashimi."

"Right!"

"I think it's great how you and your family dressed in the same fabric. It looks so rich." Kiko admires my family's coordinating clothing, "Your family looks in harmony."

Excitedly I explain that we are representing the African tradition of dressing alike for special occasions.

Standing at the entrance to the auditorium, a couple of students are offering face masks. "Would you like one?", they ask. We politely decline. Dad curiously comments, "That's something new."

Stepping into the crowded multipurpose room, a kaleidoscope of sounds coming from people speaking different languages, and the blaring multicultural music. I'm pumped with excitement.

I'm thinking, "Dang, too bad we didn't think of bringing our Bluetooth."

The aroma of good smelling food makes my stomach growl. I wish I could eat now!

As I look around, everybody is busily setting up their tables. Some with miniature flags and statues. The tables are labeled with names and numbers. Mom points to the table with the white sheet of paper attached to it, Bendle #5. Dad parks the wagon loaded with the food, next to our table. Mom reaches into a brown paper Safeway bag, and pulls out the King Tut tablecloth. Dad takes one end, and she takes the other. They carefully cover the table with the cloth, ensuring that it's perfectly centered.

Looking at me, Mom points to the rectangular shaped power strip behind the table telling me, "Plug in the crockpot please." While bending over to plug it in, I hear my name called. When I stand and look around, I see Maria. She's waving and walking towards me. I decide to meet her halfway. She's wearing a cream-colored dress with the biggest sleeves I've ever seen. She looks like she's gliding with wings.

We greet, "Hi Kyndle."
"Hi Maria, nice fit. You look sharp."
"Thanks, so do you."
"Thanks."
Glowing, Maria explains, "I'm wearing a traditional Filipino dress called a terno."
"Wow! The huge sleeves are cool."

We stroll through the crowded room back to my table. Maria greets my parents, "Hi Mr. and Mrs. Bendle."
"Hello Sweetie." Mom replies.
Dad greets Maria, "Hi ya doin' young lady?"
"I'm fine, thank you, sir."
"Good, glad to hear it."
"Can I help, Mrs. Bendle?"
"No thank you sweetie, is your table ready?"

"Yes, I finished helping my mom."

"Well in that case, if you don't mind helping Kyndle decorate our table?"

"It's no problem Mrs. Bendle."

Mom hands us tape and 8x10 photos of historical figures: Civil Rights Leader, Dr. Martin Luther King Jr., Supreme Court Justice, Thurgood Marshall, Abolitionist, Frederick Douglass, Vice President, Kamala Harris, President Barack Obama, Justice, Ketanji Brown Jackson, Poet, Amanda Gorman and Filmmaker, Tyler Perry. As we taped the photos along the edge of the table, Mom pulls out two small flags from the Safeway bag, one American flag (red, white and blue) and one Pan-African flag (red, black and green). She places them in the center of the table, before she displays our banquet of food.

When Maria and I finish taping the photos she tells Mom, "Something smells good! What did you cook, Mrs. Bendle?"

"We all cooked. Mr. Bendle made salmon croquettes, I cooked greens, cornbread, black-eye peas, okra & tomatoes, yams and Kyndle's grandmother made the sweet potato pies."

"Geez, that's a lot of food. I can't wait to try some."

"We have lots to choose from and want everyone to taste a variety of foods. Especially if they never tried some of our traditional cuisine."

"I hope I'm the first in line, and I want you to taste my family's food too. I don't want you to miss out on my mom's delicious lumpia and chicken adobo, so I'll make a plate for you and Mr. Bendle, and I'll bring it to you."

"You are so thoughtful, thank you! We look forward to tasting your mother's cooking."

Just then, Miss Fatona announces, "Class time to line up."

Maria and I begin to head over when my dad says, "Break a leg."

Our look of confusion prompts Dad to explain, "It means, good luck on stage."

Maria and I look at each other; then as if on point, we say, "Thanks."

As Maria and I head toward our classmates, I say, "Hey, I haven't seen Tinah."

"Me either. Wonder where she is."

 At that moment, I send her a text. "WYA?" She doesn't reply.

 Maria tries texting, "Tinah, where you at?" Still no reply.

Reaching the group, we both ask, "Have y'all heard from Tinah?"

Moving his head left to right, Fola silently answers. Kiko says, "No," and Jose says, "N'all man, wonder what's up with her."

Miss Fatona stands before us and notices Tinah missing, "Have any of you heard from Tinah?'

We all say, "No." in unison.

Miss Fatona looks disappointed when she says, "The show must go on, and we'll start in exactly ten minutes. Follow me."

We follow Miss Fatona backstage where she instructs us, "Line up as I call your name."

Looking at her list, she calls Tinah's name first, "Oops, she's not here, Kiko you'll go first instead." My name is called last.

After we line up, Mr. C.J. Sharpe, the attendance clerk, comes backstage and hands a note to Miss Fatona. He speaks to her in a very low tone.

She nods her head, and whispers something back to him.

He leaves.

Miss Fatona goes onstage and begins tapping the microphone to get everyone's attention. "Please be seated." She begins, "Before our program starts, I've been asked to make an important announcement."

Reading from the paper handed to her by Mr. C.J., she announces, "The World Health Organization declared the COVID19 outbreak a global health emergency. As fears escalate across California about the potential outbreak of the virus, our district has announced that effective Monday, we will begin offering a two-tiered system of in-person and Zoom classes. Thus far our school has not been notified of any confirmed cases; however, we do have some students out due to illnesses. Additionally, Antoine Thur, California State Superintendent of Public Instruction, has notified all districts of the following CDC mandates. Families choosing in-person learning for their students will be required to wear a face mask before entering the campus. COVID cases are increasing across the country, and we must take necessary measures to keep our community safe. With that said, I apologize for the timing of this grim announcement. Our primary goal is the health and safety of our students and community at large. So, without further ado, let's begin our program."

IDK!

A few parents try to ask questions, but Miss Fatona says, "Please hold your questions until after our program. Our students have worked hard to put together today's presentations, and they are anxiously waiting to present to you. Let's enjoy them, shall we?"

Pulling back the heavy velvet curtain, I see people getting up from their seats and flocking to the entry door for face masks.

Miss Fatona comes back, and we quickly line up again.

Maria softly asked, "Do you think Tinah caught the 'rona?"

Krishna says, "Maybe Covid?" not realizing Rona is slang for Coronavirus, also called Covid-19. They're the same.

A few of us shrug our shoulders, but nobody answers out loud.

"Miss Fatona simply states, let's hope Tinah is well, and that we are too. If any of us has been exposed, we will receive notification, and be required to quarantine for fourteen days. Now let's focus on why we are here. Kiko, you're up!"

Miss Fatona returns to the stage.

14

THE SPEECHES
Wednesday

Backstage my cellphone buzzes. Miss Fatona is on stage tapping the microphone to get everyone's attention.

"I see many of you have decided to put on a face mask. I wish we had them in multiple colors so that you could match your beautiful outfits.

While she talks, I check my cell.

 It's Tinah, her text says, Good luck Kyndle, I wish I could be there. My mom caught rona and I must quarantine for 14 days. I'm so bummed. 😞

 'You lie! Sorry to hear that Tinah, how are you feeling? Did you catch it?'

"No, I tested negative, I just have a really bad cold. Since my mother caught it, and my dad and I were exposed to her, we have to quarantine. It's messed up! I'm so bummed. I really wanted to give my speech with y'all."

I'll let Miss Fatona know and I hope your mother gets better soon!

Miss Fatona probably knows by now; my dad just called the school. He said the secretary scheduled a Zoom meeting for me with Miss Fatona.

It's good you still get to give your speech, but it's too bad it has to be over Zoom." We're starting soon so I'll hit you later.

K.

Miss Fatona is still talking to the audience, "My heartfelt thanks go out to all of you for preparing the bountiful meal we will enjoy following today's program. I must say, you've all made this occasion very special with your decorated tables, beautiful attire and if the food tastes as good as it smells, I know we are all in for a treat."

Miss Fatona continues, "International Day happens once a year here at Michelle Obama Academy. This is a time we recognize and honor diverse cultures. Thank you for all your contributions. Please give a nice welcome to our first presenter, Kiko Akita."

I want to tell Maria and the others what Tinah said in her text, but I think I should wait to see if Miss Fatona mentions it.

Kiko enters the stage, and the audience applauds. Her embroidered dress shimmers in the lights. I'm unable to focus on what she's saying as I'm nervously praying everything goes well for me. My mind wonders, as I think of all sorts of things that could happen, like tripping and falling before reaching the microphone or drawing a blank and standing there looking dumbfounded. I keep telling myself not to have negative thoughts, yet they keep creeping into my mind. The next thing I hear is thunderous applause. Krishna's up next. He's peeking through the curtain and lets us know Kiko is taking her bow. She returns backstage beaming with joy!

Before Krishna goes on stage, I take another peek at the audience and see my grandparents wearing masks sitting with my parents. They have on the same beautiful clothing my parents and I are wearing. My family looks so sharp.

Sitting directly behind my parents is Krishna's family. His mother is wearing a beautiful powder-blue sari with silver trim. The bracelets she's wearing practically cover her arm. Krishna's dad is wearing the same color as his mom.

Scanning the room from behind the curtain, I can see Jose's parents; they are wearing ponchos.

Turning to Jose I comment, "Hey Jose, that's a cool poncho your dad has on. Who's the Black dude on the poncho?"

"He's a Mexican warrior, Cuauhtémoc [kwaw'temok], the Aztec emperor."

"Wow, he reminds me of my grandad."

Speech after speech, the crowd erupts in applause, laughter, and sometimes tears. Maria takes her bow, and the crowd continues to cheer and whistle when she comes backstage. Everyone is smiling and hugging with elation and relief. They're done. I'm not. It's time for me to go onstage.

Miss Fatona announces, "Now for our final presenter."

Markie approaches me and we dap, with our special handshake before I go onstage.

Maria is grinning ear to ear as she walks directly to me. The audience is still applauding when she says, "It's not so bad once you get up there. You got this!"

I have no time to respond to her comment, but I know she's right. I got this!

Like we all did, my classmates stand backstage peeking through the curtain, watching and listening.

Standing confidently with my head held high, I walk to the center of the stage and stand in front of the microphone that's directly beneath my neck. Maria is much shorter than I am. Just as I am about to adjust the microphone, Miss Fatona returns to the stage to adjust the stand for me, bringing the mic to the perfect level. The queasiness I felt earlier in my belly doesn't return. I'm feeling good!

I know I have the support of my village on and offstage. Like my dad always tells me, fail to prepare, prepare to fail. I've prepared, and I will not fail. I take a deep breath before I begin reading from my paper: "'Lead me. Guide me along the way.' I can imagine my ancestors singing words similar to these as they made the long journey from Africa to the Americas."

The audience is captivated, with all eyes on me. My head lowers while I look at my speech, and nervousness creeps back in. I look at my parents before continuing. At this moment I decide to speak from my heart, not from my prepared speech. I pause briefly before speaking, "I knew I wanted to share delicious food from my culture, but I couldn't decide on a dish, so my mother and I decided to write on my permission slip, 'Soul food dish.' Later, when permission slips were turned in, Miss Fatona asked us to state the origin of the food we plan to bring. I was the only person in class who could not answer her question. It was a very embarrassing moment for me.

I was feeling down, and my mom sensed something was wrong. When she pressed me to tell her what was going on, 'Did something happen at school?' I told her how badly I felt being the only person in my class who could not state the origin of my cultural food. Today I'm proud to explain the origin of my cultural food."

"Ahem, ahem." I cleared my throat again, "I'll bet most of you have eaten foods that were brought to America during the slave trade.

I pause.

If you've ever eaten watermelon, collard greens, okra, or black-eyed peas you've digested foods that originate from Africa. I'll bet you didn't know, the West African kola nut traveled to America on slave ships and was once a main ingredient in Coke a-Cola. The nuts have twice as much caffeine as coffee. They were used to suppress the appetite of enslaved people. If you're wondering how and why these foods got to America from Africa, I'm about to explain.

During the middle passage voyage, it was important to the capturers to keep the enslaved alive. Although roughly two million captured died during the voyage, those survivors were feed what they were accustomed to eating, to help prevent them from dying. So, foods from Africa were loaded onto the ships and traveled with the enslaved people. Keep in mind, the capturers couldn't get paid if the cargo (slaves) died. These foods eventually made their way into homes across America.

The fact that my friends could name the origin of their foods so easily and I could not, bothered me. Now I understand why the question was so difficult for me.

My friends, who have lineage from countries like Mexico, Japan, Philippines, and Europe, all easily answered Miss Fatona's question. The more they answered, I realized that I was more familiar with the origin of their foods, than I was with my own.

Before this assignment, I'd never really thought about where my cultural food comes from. I was baffled because the name 'Soul food' doesn't connect this cuisine to my country or any other country.

Through my research, I learned that the enslaved were mostly from West Africa. My great-great-great-great-grandparents are Native Black Americans, yet our cultural food is not called American. My ancestors were creating cuisine in America, since the first enslaved Africans arrived in 1619, long before the opening of Ellis Island, where many new immigrants entered this country in the late 1800's introducing their cuisines.

My dad told me sometimes it takes a village, well my village includes relatives, neighbors, and friends, who taught me that Black

Americans gave the word 'Soul' a new meaning in the 1960s. During that time, Black people named their cultural food 'Soul food.' Some say the name connects us to our ancestors because, like the Soul, it never dies.

In our early history, enslaved people didn't have the freedom to learn to read and write English. Recipes were shared by word of mouth. Those who learned to read English did so secretly because it was against the law for an enslaved person to be educated.

Soul food was created from scraps my ancestors were given, coupled with foods brought from Africa. Throughout the Southern United States of America, the hands of the enslaved prepared meals for the slaveholders. In fact, two very famous chefs of their time were Hercules Posey, an enslaved chief cook for President George Washington and James Hemings, an enslaved chef for President Thomas Jefferson. These cooks set the tone for American cuisine. American Blacks have run the White House kitchen as chefs, butlers, stewards and servers for every first family for nearly 150 years. In recent years, chef Andre Rush has cooked meals for past Presidents: Bill Clinton, George Bush, Barack Obama, and Donald Trump.

Today people often refer to Soul food as Southern cuisine or comfort food. My family still proudly calls it Soul food.

As it turns out, there is no easy answer to why my cultural food is not named 'American food.' My parents and grandparents were the first members of my village to help me to understand why. What I've learned in the past week has given me a special pride for my cultural food. Pride that I didn't have before.

Soul food cuisine was introduced to American Southern colonies during the slavery era. The type of cuisine prepared by enslaved people depended on the region they lived in. Soul food in Louisiana has African and French influences. Soul food from the Carolinas has African and Spanish influences. African cooking techniques were introduced into plantation homes. After the slaveholders took the best parts of the pig: ham and ribs. Scraps were rationed that included feet, tails, ears, and intestines. These scraps were used by early American Black People to create delicious meals for their families.

Before researching for this speech, I had no idea cotton was not the main crop picked by the enslaved. Every movie I ever watched about slavery, told a story of slaves picking cotton. I now know one of the first crops cultivated by the enslaved people was rice. Enslaved people worked the fields, harvesting sugar, coffee, tobacco, fruits, cocoa, and cotton. Their forced free labor made many people in this country and countries all over the world very rich.

A typical meal was made in one pot, using vegetables from small gardens, seafood they caught, meats they trapped and hunted and scraps that the slaveholder didn't want.

Today some of the best-known one-pot meals are gumbo, jambalaya, and crawfish étouffée. The rice, meat, seafood, and vegetables are all cooked together in the same pot. These dishes have lots of African influence. I bet you didn't know that American sweet potatoes resemble African yams. My ancestors called sweet potatoes 'yams,' and the name stuck!

In our culture, New Year's Day is celebrated with certain foods: greens like collards represent dollar bills, black-eyed peas a symbol of coins, and cornbread represents bricks of gold. I know many people consider pork to be unhealthy meat, but for my ancestors who toiled the soil, those scraps of pig's feet, tails, neck bones, and other rationed parts provided the protein needed for survival. Many native Black Americans still eat pork and black-eyed peas every New Year's Day for good luck. I can say with pride that the origin of my cultural food is America! Soul food is American food!"

The booming applause is deafening. People are roaring, standing, and whistling as I bow. Finally, I stand proudly with the widest grin plastered on my face. I nailed it!

Miss Fatona, and my classmates join me on stage. We all hold hands and take a collective bow. Lifting my head, I can't help smiling at all the people in their beautiful spectrum of colors as we all savor and appreciate our standing ovations.

Speaking to the audience, Miss Fatona leans into the microphone, "I am so very proud of my students. They've made me so happy. She turns to look at us, and says, "You've done a phenomenal job!"

More applause erupts from the audience, and Miss Fatona says, "Let us feast!"

Backstage we are smiling, laughing, dapping and high fiving when Miss Fatona congratulates us all, stating, "Y'all nailed it! This Day will be ranked among the best ever!" When she has finished speaking, Fola approaches me with his arm extended and hand balled into a fist to connect with mine. We pound and he says, "Low key, you did that, brah."

My response, "Yeah, guess I did answer that!"

Fola responds, "Fa sho!"

With a broad grin, Miss Fatona encourages us, "Go join your families, there are lots of folks out there waiting to congratulate you! Kyndle, can I see you for a minute?"

Super charged with high energy and uncontained excitement, my extremely energetic friends exit backstage to join their families. Within seconds, Miss Fatona and I are the only two left backstage. She turns to me and says, "Thank you for speaking from your heart. That speech was fantastic. I learned so much from you!"

She hugs me.

I thank her, before taking off to join my family. Next, I remember to tell her, "Tinah is okay. She's not sick, it's her mother."

"I know, but thanks anyway for telling me, she'll have a chance to give her speech. I got her!"

ABOUT THE AUTHOR

Ramona Thomas is an author of educational and realistic fiction targeting young readers. A California native, she was born, raised, and resides in the San Francisco Bay Area. She first wrote "Grandma's Brown Cookies," later renamed "Doctor Wizmagic's Potion," a story about a boy who learns to make healthier food choices and discovers that organic brown foods are better for him. In collaboration with Yvetta "Doll" Franklin, she co-authored "The Code Switch," a delightful story about two best girlfriends who compete to become valedictorian. "IDK!" Is a realistic work of historical fiction about Soul food in America and a young boy's quest to learn about his ethnic cuisine. Thomas received her Master of Education from Holy Names University.

Her motto: "Aspire to Inspire!"

DISCUSSION QUESTIONS

Do you know the origin of your cultural food?

What fruits and vegetables grow in the region where you live?

Does Maria think Soul food is from Korea?

Why do Kyndle's classmates josh him when he doesn't answer the question?

How would you feel if you were Kyndle?

What kind of relationship does Kyndle have with his mother?

What kind of relationship does Kyndle have with his father?

Can you name a tradition Kyndle's family practiced before eating?

Do you have any experience with going to church?

How does your church compare to the churches Kyndle describes?

Do you think Kyndle's dad was going to clean the kitchen?

Do you think Kyndle's mom should have been upset when his dad didn't immediately wash the dishes?

IDK!

What did you learn about Native Black American culture?

Who was your favorite character and why?

Why is Kyndle's cultural food called Soul food?

Do you think the name Soul food should be changed to something else? If so, what?

Before reading this story, did you know anything about American Soul food?

What was the promise of 40 acres and a mule?

Who are Aboriginal Americans?

What happened after Christopher Columbus arrived in America?

Why does Kyndle's grandad suggest he look things up, and do his research?

What group of people benefited most from the Homestead Act of 1862?

Between 1870 and 1900 where did most of the immigrants migrate from?

How do your family traditions compare to Kyndle's?

KYNDLE'S FAMILY RECIPES

Southern Salmon Croquettes

This salmon croquette recipe, an African American and southern food favorite, is simple and easy to prepare. Depending on your family history, you may know salmon croquettes by another name, such as salmon patties or salmon cakes. The names may be slightly different, but one thing remains the same: they're delicious.

Ingredients:

1 can (15 ½ ounce) pink or red salmon
1 medium onion, finely chopped
½ cup finely chopped bell pepper, red or green
2 large eggs, beaten
½ cup yellow cornmeal
2 tablespoons of butter or extra virgin olive oil
Salt and pepper to taste

Instructions:

In a medium bowl, drain the juice from the can of salmon, and use a fork to break the salmon apart into small pieces. Sprinkle with cornmeal. Add bell peppers, sweet onion, seasonings, Worcestershire sauce, olive oil, and beaten eggs. Mix until well combined. Shape into about four patties. Heat butter or oil in a large skillet over medium-high heat. Once the skillet is hot, cook the patties for three to five minutes on each side or until they are a golden-brown color.

COLLARD GREENS

Ingredients:
1 teaspoon of red pepper flakes or jalapeño pepper, chopped 4 bunches of collard greens (or 2 bags, precut and cleaned) Salt and pepper White wine vinegar to taste
1 medium sweet onion, chopped
Fully cooked turkey necks, smoked turkey leg, or ham hock
Optional: 2–3 garlic cloves, garlic powder, onion powder, or seasoned salt

Instructions:
Remove the collard green leaves from the stem. Wash the collards several times in cold water to remove any dirt and grit. You can also use salt to help remove the grit if needed. Rinse well and set aside. In a large pot, add a tablespoon of olive oil and the chopped onions and garlic. Sauté until tender. Add seasoning to taste; choose some or all of these: garlic powder, onion powder, salt, Lawry's seasoned salt, pepper, and/or white wine vinegar. Add in red pepper flakes or chopped jalapeño pepper. Remove seeds for less heat. Add turkey leg, turkey necks, or ham hock. Only add enough water to cover the meat; too much water makes the dish soupy. Bring to a boil, and then reduce heat to simmer for about thirty to sixty minutes. Meat should be falling off the bone. This helps the broth take on that delicious flavor! Add in the collard greens. Simmer covered for about forty-five minutes to an hour or until your desired tenderness is reached. The leaves should become dark green. You can increase the heat if needed, but do not boil the collard greens. They will wilt down as they cook.

SWEET POTATO PIE

Use yams, which in the United States are still called sweet potatoes. Choose the red-skinned sweet potatoes with orange-colored flesh.

Ingredients:
1 unbaked pie shell
2–3 yams
2–3 medium eggs
½ cup evaporated milk
1 tablespoon pure vanilla extract
1 teaspoon ground cinnamon (optional)
½ teaspoon ground nutmeg
¼ teaspoon ground ginger (optional)
1 cup granulated sugar
½ cup brown sugar
1 stick of real butter (no imitation)

Instructions:
Pierce two to three potatoes with a fork. Use a foil-lined cookie sheet to bake them until sugar oozes out of the skin, about fifty to sixty-five minutes at 350°F. Peel potato skins when yams are cool, and place peeled yams in a medium-size mixing bowl. Blend yams until strings are wrapped around beaters. Rinse beaters and continue blending. Make sure your mixture is not stringy. Add a melted stick of real butter, then add nutmeg, ginger, and/or cinnamon. (Taste mixture and add more to taste.) Add eggs and blend. Blend in sugar. (Taste and add more if desired.) Add evaporated milk, vanilla extract, and melted butter. Whisk until the mixture

is creamy and airy. Bake the pie shell for seven to ten minutes at 325°F.

Remove the shell from the oven, then turn the heat up to 350°F. Start adding the sweet potato pie filling into the pie shell and smooth it out. Bake the pie for forty-five minutes to an hour. Let the pie cool until it is at room temperature.

Enjoy!

BLACK-EYED PEAS

Ingredients:
1 16-ounce package of black-eyed peas (you may use frozen peas alternatively)
1 cooked ham hock or smoked turkey leg
8–12 cups of water (enough to cover the meat)
1¼ cups onion, chopped
1 cup celery, chopped
1 teaspoon salt
⅛ teaspoon cayenne pepper
1 bay leaf

Instructions:
Soak dry peas overnight (no need to soak frozen peas). Rinse peas before cooking. Use a large dutch oven or soup pot. Place meat (ham hock or smoked turkey) into the pot, and cover with water. Add chopped onion, celery, and bay leaf. Simmer meat and veggies in water until meat begins to fall off the bone. Add black-eyed peas to the pot; simmer for about one hour. Add fresh or frozen okra, and cook for fifteen to twenty minutes. When the peas are nice and creamy, remove the bay leaf before serving.

CORNBREAD

Ingredients:
1 cup Albers white or yellow cornmeal
1 cup all-purpose flour
¼ cup granulated sugar
1 tablespoon baking powder
1 teaspoon salt
1 cup milk
⅓ cup vegetable oil
1 large egg, lightly beaten

Instructions:
Preheat oven to 400°F. Grease an eight-inch-square baking pan. Combine meal, flour, sugar, baking powder, and salt in a medium-sized bowl. Combine milk, oil, and egg in a small bowl; mix well. Add milk mixture to flour mixture; stir just until blended. Pour into prepared pan. Bake for twenty to twenty-five minutes or until a wooden pick inserted in the center comes out clean. Serve warm.

Notes:
Recipe may be doubled. Use a greased thirteen-by-nine-inch baking pan; bake as above.

For muffins: Spoon the batter into ten to twelve greased or paper-lined muffin cups, filling two-thirds of the way full. Bake in a preheated 400°F oven for fifteen minutes.

RED BEANS AND RICE

Ingredients:
1 pound dry red beans
2 teaspoons cooking oil
14 ounces Louisiana hot links or andouille sausage
1 yellow onion
1 green bell pepper
3 ribs celery
4 cloves garlic
2 teaspoons smoked paprika
1 teaspoon dried oregano
1 teaspoon dried thyme
½ teaspoon garlic powder
½ teaspoon onion powder
¼ teaspoon cayenne pepper
¼ teaspoon black pepper, freshly cracked
2 bay leaves
6 cups water
¼ cup parsley, chopped
1 tablespoon salt, or to taste
1½ cups long-grain white rice (uncooked)
3 green onions
Ham hock

Instructions:
The night before, add the dry beans to a large bowl with double their volume in water. Allow the beans to soak overnight. Beans

should double in size after soaking, and most of the water should be absorbed. Add ham hock to a large pot; cover with water. When water boils, lower to simmer for about an hour. Add seasoning to the pot with ham hock (smoked paprika, dried oregano, dried thyme, garlic powder, onion powder, cayenne pepper, and cracked black pepper). Slice hot links in round circles. Chop onions, celery, and bell pepper. Mince garlic cloves. Drain and rinse the soaked beans. Add them to the pot along with the water and chopped veggies. Give the pot a brief stir to blend the ingredients. Place a lid on the pot, turn the heat up to medium-high, and bring it up to a boil. Once boiling, turn the heat down to medium-low, and let the pot boil for one hour, stirring occasionally. Replace the lid every time you stir. After boiling for one hour, the beans should be tender. Using a ladle or large cup, scoop out two to three ladles or cups of beans. Smash the beans until they become a thick paste. Put the smashed beans back into the pot and stir. While the beans are simmering for their final thirty minutes, cook the rice. Add the rice and three cups of water to a sauce pot. Place a lid on top, turn the heat on to high, and bring it up to a boil. Once it is boiling, turn the heat down to low, and let the rice simmer for fifteen minutes. After fifteen minutes, turn the heat off, and let the rice rest for five minutes without removing the lid. Fluff the rice with a fork before serving. Once the red beans have thickened, taste the red beans and add salt to your liking. Start with a dash, and add more as needed. Serve the red beans in a bowl topped with a scoop of rice and a sprinkle of sliced green onions to garnish.

OKRA AND TOMATOES

Ingredients:
4 slices bacon
1 onion, chopped
3 cups sliced okra (fresh or frozen, fresh preferred)
1½-ounce can diced tomatoes
2–4 Roma tomatoes
1 tablespoon paprika
1 tablespoon salt
1 tablespoon garlic powder
1 tablespoon black pepper
1 tablespoon onion powder
1 tablespoon cayenne pepper
1 tablespoon dried oregano
1 tablespoon dried thyme

Instructions:
Slice smoked bacon into one-inch pieces. Blend seasoning together (paprika, salt, garlic powder, black pepper, cayenne pepper, dried oregano, and dried thyme). Dice fresh okra into round pieces. Dice onion. Score the tip of Roma tomato, and boil for eight to ten minutes. Remove Roma tomatoes from the pot, and place in a bowl of cold water or ice to cool. Once cooled, peel skin from the tomatoes. Chop the Roma tomatoes. In a heavy-bottomed sauté pan over medium-high heat, add thick-cut smoked bacon. Cook until they are crisp, and the pan is nicely coated with oil from the bacon. Add the onion and sauté until tender, about three

minutes. Add the okra, Roma tomatoes, and canned tomatoes, making sure to add the reserved juice from the tomatoes to the sauté pan. Add seasoning one tablespoon at a time to taste. Simmer until okra is tender.

RICE

Ingredients:
2 cups water (optional: use chicken broth instead)
4 cups of liquid for brown rice
1/2 teaspoon salt
1 tablespoon butter or oil (optional)
1 cup long-grain white rice (optional: use brown rice instead)

Instructions:
Bring the liquid to a boil in a medium saucepan. Add the salt and butter and allow the butter to melt. When the liquid has returned to a boil, stir in the rice. Let the water return to a light simmer. Stir again, cover the pot, and turn the heat down to low. Keep the rice simmering slightly, and keep the pot covered (you may have to peek after a few minutes to make sure the heat is at the correct temperature, but then let it cook covered). Start checking to see if the rice is tender and all of the liquid is absorbed at about seventeen minutes. It may take up to twenty-five, especially if you are making a larger quantity of rice. Most packages of brown rice will say to boil for longer than white rice, so for around thirty to thirty-five minutes. When the rice is cooked, turn off the heat, and let it sit for another couple of minutes to finish absorbing any liquid. Take off the lid, fluff the rice with a fork, and let it sit for another two minutes or so, so that some of the excess moisture in the rice dries off. If you are using a rice cooker, follow the instructions provided.

HOT WATER CORN BREAD

Ingredients:
1 cup cornmeal
1 teaspoon salt
1 teaspoon white sugar
1 tablespoon shortening
¾ cup boiling water

Instructions:
In a medium bowl, combine cornmeal, salt, and sugar. Add boiling water and shortening; stir until shortening melts. Pour oil or bacon fat to a depth of a half inch in a large skillet and heat to 375°F. (Shape cornmeal mixture into flattened balls using a heaping tablespoon as a measuring guide.) Fry each in hot oil, turning once, until crisp and golden brown, about five minutes. Drain on paper towels. Serve at once with maple syrup or honey.

www.ingramcontent.com/pod-product-compliance
Lightning Source LLC
LaVergne TN
LVHW041844070526
838199LV00045BA/1434